BBC
DOCTOR WHO
IN THE
BLOOD

BBC

DOCTOR WHO
IN THE
BLOOD

JENNY T. COLGAN

BOOKS

1 3 5 7 9 10 8 6 4 2

BBC Books, an imprint of Ebury Publishing
20 Vauxhall Bridge Road,
London SW1V 2SA

BBC Books is part of the Penguin Random House group of
companies whose addresses can be found at
global.penguinrandomhouse.com

Penguin
Random House
UK

Doctor Who is a BBC Wales production for BBC One
Executive producers: Steven Moffat and Brian Minchin

First published by BBC Books in 2016
Paperback edition published in 2017

www.penguin.co.uk

A CIP catalogue record for this book is available from
the British Library

ISBN 9781785941115

Editorial Director: Albert DePetrillo
Series Consultant: Justin Richards
Editor: Kate Fox
Production: Alex Goddard

Printed and bound in Great Britain by Clays Ltd, St Ives PLC

Penguin Random House is committed to a sustainable future for our
business, our readers and our planet. This book is made from
Forest Stewardship Council® certified paper.

MIX
Paper from
responsible sources
FSC® C018179

Chapter
One

Donna hurled down her phone in frustration.

'Your call is important to us...' came the recorded voice on the other end of the line.

'Well, it isn't, is it?' said Donna into the speaker. 'Because if it *was*, you wouldn't have *that robot* repeating that at me for *forty-five minutes*. What do you do with unimportant calls? Send them electric shocks?'

'So, this is fun and everything,' said the Doctor, glancing up from where he was busying himself at the other side of the TARDIS console. 'But could you possibly hang up and explain yourself? You've been buried in that phone ever since you got asked to leave the spa... almost as if you were avoiding me.'

Donna turned her head to hide the fact that she was blushing. The Doctor's mouth twitched.

'I'm not!' said Donna. 'I just have to get through to my bank to cancel my credit card. Except the *idiots* aren't picking up.'

There was a long pause whilst the TARDIS wheezed a little, as if to cover up any embarrassment.

'Come on. What did you do? Tell me!' said the Doctor.

Donna put down the phone and folded her arms. 'It was all a big misunderstanding.'

The Doctor took off his glasses and gave her a look. 'It's a spa, Donna. What's to misunderstand? Lie down, get smeared with... I don't know, *goo*... put bits of you in different temperatures of water...'

'You have no idea what goes on at a spa, do you?'

'None at all. Wish people would stop giving me the vouchers.' He straightened up. 'Anyway, could you explain to me why we just had to leave one? In a hurry?'

'Well, I was having this massage, right... stripped down—'

'I don't need every *single* detail.'

'No, listen, right. I was having a massage by this robot, and it was dead good, and normally in spas you tip the staff so I thought maybe I should tip it, and there was a slot, and...'

'You put your *credit card* in it?'

'It had very powerful and firm robotty fingers!'

'You inserted a magnetic strip into a magnetron robot?'

'If their stupid robots blow up if you stick tiny bits inside them, they should come with a warning sign!'

'*You* should come with a warning sign.'

Donna sighed and hung up the bleeping phone. 'Well, it was *not* relaxing. Maybe I should go see my friends.'

'Thought you didn't like your friends.'

'I don't like *Nerys*. The rest of them are all right. Yeah. Mates. That's what I need.'

The Doctor looked slightly wounded. 'I'm your mate.'

Donna looked at him. 'Of course you are, dumbo. OK, right, the nine best things about Lee were…'

'Actually,' said the Doctor glancing down at the dials. 'I was thinking of popping by Earth, as it happens. Kate Bush is playing live. This is rarer than the fourth phase rising of the nineteen golden Osirius horned moons. And every bit as glorious.'

Chapter
Two

'Who do you think you are, you cow? Wind your fat neck in.'

Alan's fingers rattled happily off the keys as he pressed 'send' and sat back in contentment. That would show her.

Now, wasn't there another young actress who'd been in the papers showing rather too much flesh, in Alan's opinion. He could go and point that out in the comments section.

He took a handful of cheese puffs in one hand then scratched his armpit. With his other hand he clicked on his filthy mouse.

He felt a draft, but ignored it. Was probably making the motor run too much again. Stupid computer.

It felt cold in the room, though. Alan rarely felt the cold – with his bulk he was generally too warm rather than the opposite – but there was a definite chill in the air, as if someone had left a window open.

He spun round. Nothing. His mother was out. There shouldn't be anyone around. There wasn't. He liked to do this kind of thing alone.

He told himself not to be daft and turned back to open windows on his computer screen.

Alan liked to think he wasn't afraid of anything; not afraid of putting his opinions out there, not afraid to tell celebrities the truth, as he saw it. Of course he didn't sign his name to it; he wasn't that stupid. But they made him so angry. He started again.

But before he'd got far, Alan felt a draft in the room. A cold draft. He felt the hairs go up at the back of his neck. Goosebumps raised themselves on his arm.

His computer froze.

He pounded the keyboard in fury. 'Come on! Come on, you useless piece of garbage… come on.'

Suddenly, he felt an icy finger. Inside.

It pushed at his heart. Right inside. He felt it flip, push his heart over, and then, suddenly, a cold, cold hand began to squeeze.

Alan shouted out loud in horror. And then, something deeper came over him: he felt furious, enraged beyond anything. He picked up the keyboard, hurled it at the wall, followed by the chair. He screamed and yelled, pounding around; his fist went into the mirror in his frenzy of rage.

His dirty sweatpants snagged on the corner of the desk and he turned, to roar, but it was too late: he clutched at his chest, and abruptly fell over, making a noise like a crashing tree.

He tried to scream out for his mother; but she was out and besides, he had no more breath. Instead he could only gulp furiously, like a fish, his eyes struggling to focus on anything other than the dusty jumble of wires and cables like sleeping snakes, malevolently coiled around his bedroom floor, as he heaved his final breath, and his eyes saw nothing more.

The computer whooshed back into life. It made several beeping noises and a blue light flashed as a current rippled through it. Then, everything was silent.

Chapter
Three

'Hettie!'

Donna dropped her suitcase and opened her arms. Hettie was standing in her pristine Chiswick doorway. She lived in one of the posh houses, down by the riverside.

She'd come a long way, thought Donna, since they had started out together at Belmont Primary. Then Hettie had been hilarious and wild and always up to mischief of one sort or another, egged on by Donna, and it had been that way all through their mad teenage years.

Then Hettie's husband Cam had got a big job, and now she was incredibly stressed all the time and always having to go off for yoga retreats and needing lots of people to help her out with stuff and cleaners and nannies and things, which seemed to Donna a pretty stressful thing to do rather than just looking after your own kids, but that wasn't something people with children particularly liked to hear, so she just left it.

But the old Hettie had to be in there somewhere, right? Always up with a ridiculous crack or a filthy remark about someone… That would help.

'Het!'

Hettie looked at her wearily. She had become incredibly thin, and it made her look really tired and anxious. She was clasping her phone and merely glanced up at Donna before jabbing something out on it.

'It's been too long!' Donna worried slightly that she wasn't 100 per cent sure how long it actually had been – 'More or less about the same time,' the Doctor had said. 'Don't worry, you're not here or anything.'

'Why would I be here?' Donna had said. 'I travel with you.'

There'd been a short pause then, and she'd known not to push it.

'Yeah,' said Hettie, still pressing buttons, and there was a short, uncomfortable pause. 'Well, you coming in then?'

Hettie's house was spotless; immaculate. There wasn't a sound to be heard.

'Where are the kids?' Donna asked brightly. She loved the twins; their black hair fell in dark ringlets and they were a blur of constant movement.

Hettie shrugged. 'Kumon maths. Then karate, then Mandarin. Then tutorials.'

Donna put her bag down. Hettie didn't put her phone down.

'Hets, they're six years old.'

'Exactly,' said Hettie. 'I'm already too late to get them in to tennis. I can't believe it.'

Donna frowned. 'Where's Cam?'

Cam was Hettie's high-level husband. Well, he was high level now. He'd never been high level before; he'd just been a lazy, sweet average sort of a bloke who'd kind of turned up at the right time when Hettie had decided she wanted to get married and they'd kind of fallen into it, and Donna had always thought he was really easy-going and nice, but then suddenly everything had got very busy and important at work for him and that was that, she barely saw him again.

Hettie rolled her eyes. 'Oh, it's Cameron now. He doesn't answer to Cam any more. Too busy and important. He's at work. He's always at bloody work. Of course. Leaving everything to me.'

A cleaner came to the door. 'All done now, Mrs Wake.'

Hettie didn't even turn round, simply shooed the cleaner away with the wave of a hand, still holding her phone. 'I don't think she can be trusted,' she said to Donna, more than loudly enough for the cleaner to hear.

The woman's back stiffened, but she didn't turn round.

'So she does the cleaning... When are you picking up the kids?'

'Oh no, the useless nanny does that,' said Hettie. 'It's about all she does.' She sighed, and laughed at something on her computer screen, which was next to her on the sofa. But not kindly.

'What is it?' said Donna.

'Oh some idiot's just said something really stupid on my messageboard… Wait for it…'

The lights on her devices flashed red.

'Oh yes, there they go, all piling in. Ha! That'll teach 'em.'

She started typing something flamboyantly fast, her greige-painted nails tapping against the keyboard, the clicking noise incredibly loud. Donna sat there awkwardly.

Finally Hettie finished whatever she was doing, and looked up at Donna as if she'd forgotten she was even there. 'Glass of wine?'

'Yeah' said Donna, hoping it might help.

'So,' said Donna, as they sat down again on the impeccably plumped cushions.

Hettie immediately picked her device up and scanned it, a scornful smile playing across her lips, as well as the occasional wince.

Donna looked around. Everything in the room matched: silver grey with purple accents everywhere. It was too neat and tidy for a normal person to have done it. 'Did you get someone else to do this room?' said Donna.

Hettie nodded. 'Blooming interior designers. Bloody thieves more like.' She resumed her typing.

Donna sipped her – clearly very expensive – wine politely. 'So… anyway, I was seeing this bloke. Kind of. And… are you busy or what?'

Hettie looked at her blankly, pulling an expensive-looking shawl around her as if she was freezing, even though it was perfectly warm in the house. Too thin, Donna found herself thinking glumly. But still, she could feel a draft.

'Sorry,' said Hettie, not sounding it. 'Just waiting on my useless bloody personal trainer to cancel as per bloody usual. I'll tell him.'

Again with the clicking.

Donna blinked. This was mad. 'Het,' she said. 'What's *wrong* with you? What's happened?'

Hettie sniffed and looked at the device again. 'I don't know what you mean.'

'This isn't you! We should be sitting up and gossiping and swapping funny stories about awful boyfriends and... not banging on about annoying "personal trainers" and posting on internet messageboards.'

There was a pause. Hettie's face changed, became stony-hard. 'Well, I find that very offensive,' she said.

'I didn't... I didn't... mean...' Not for the first time, Donna cursed the way she was too quick to speak up. 'Sorry, I didn't mean it to sound harsh.'

'I'm just saying,' said Hettie. 'I don't think it's appropriate to speak to me like that in my own home.'

'OK, OK, I'm sorry' said Donna. 'Seriously. Sheez.'

'This is my safe space,' said Hettie. 'My sanctuary.' She turned back to her handheld and started tapping buttons on it in a very passive-aggressive way, as if Donna wasn't there at all.

Donna stared at her for a moment. 'Are you all right, Het?' she said one more time, in her kindest voice.

'I'm fine,' said Hettie, not looking fine. Not looking fine at all. Her hand was at her chest, as if something was hurting her. She went back to furiously tapping buttons, not looking up.

Donna felt incredibly uneasy and not at all sure what to do. 'Um, so,' she said, shifting on her seat. 'So, I'll just... I'll maybe just...'

'Yeah, actually something's come up?' drawled Hettie, pressing 'send'. 'Sorry. Maybe you can't stay after all...'

'You know what,' said Donna, annoyed she hadn't got that in first. 'That's fine. Bye! I'll see myself out.'

Donna walked down the road, heart pounding, adrenalin surging through her system.

It was odd: she'd faced monsters – frightening ones, and touching ones – and terrible situations and grave danger in her travels with the Doctor. But, somehow, falling out with a friend felt kind of just as bad. And she wasn't sure how she felt about that.

As she walked, something pinged in Donna's pocket. It was her own device, with a message, indicating she had been 'unfriended' from all her social media accounts. Unfriended by Hettie.

She swallowed. What had she done? Had she been judge-y? Disapproving?

The old Hettie, they could have talked it over, joked, had a laugh. But the new one... She'd been so aggressive, and defensive, and had marshalled her devices around her like battlements.

Donna searched her memory. Maybe because she hadn't been in contact for a while? Maybe she hadn't clicked on enough pictures of Hettie's children. Hettie might not see them that much, but she posted a lot of pictures of them.

It felt, Donna thought as she stomped along in the cold evening, harder and harder to keep track of who was offended about things, and why. Why people kept getting themselves cross. It seemed curious, considering how much real trouble there surely was to worry about in the world.

But that didn't stop her feeling sad; didn't stop her running the friendship through her mind – all the fun they'd had at school, the mad nights out they'd shared, the laughs…

It was the oddest thing. When she'd lost Lee – well, it was heartbreaking; whether he'd been real or not, he had felt so real to her. But people understood that. They understood heartbreak and loss. Even the Doctor, Donna reckoned, understood that. Or perhaps especially him.

And you could never lose your family, though occasionally not for want of trying. Her and her mum could fight till the end of time, they'd still be each other's back-up, always there.

But losing a friend. That was different. Friends were chosen purely on personality; a shared sense of humour; a sly glance; a joy in each other's successes, uniting against anyone they felt had wronged them.

She found a cheap chain hotel by the river and checked in, hoping as she did so that her cards were working again, which they were. Then she went up to her rather basic room, and, feeling slightly ashamed, quickly had a little cry before bed, wondering if anyone ever felt truly like a proper, confident grown-up and, if they did, when would it happen for her?

Chapter
Four

Donna felt a little better in the morning. Nothing like a good cry and a fluffy towelling robe in a thin plastic bag. And two small biscuits next to a mini kettle. She took a long bubble bath and went down to breakfast still feeling puzzled and sad, but rather more resolute.

The Doctor was sitting in a wing chair in the corner, a large broadsheet newspaper covering his face.

The headline in the paper, in huge font, read 'Concerning Increase in Sedentary Deaths'. The slightly more engaging headline in the tabloid he'd already read and discarded was emblazoned 'THE TROLL HAUL – KEYBOARD WARRIOR MASSACRE'.

'Morning,' she said.

'Morning,' said the Doctor, lowering the paper with a concerned look on his face. He was wearing his glasses and a waiter had just put a vast cup of black coffee next to him.

'What have I told you about drinking coffee?'

The Doctor glanced at it guiltily. 'Best not?'

'Best not. You go Full Tigger. Give it here.'

Donna dumped plenty of milk and a single sweetener in it. Then she looked at the sweetener, sighed, and added a whole spoonful of sugar.

The Doctor frowned and looked closer. 'What's up with you?'

'What? Nothing.'

'Why aren't you staying at your friend's?'

'Because she's a cow. Shut up. How was Kate Bush?'

The Doctor's eyes went slightly misty for a moment. 'She seems to have written rather a lot of songs about my life,' he muttered gruffly. 'Although it is entirely possible everybody there thought that.' He pulled up another newspaper. 'Did you see this?'

'"Trip-Trapped Trolls",' Donna read. 'That's not a very nice headline.'

'They keep finding dead people who were… prominent on the internet. And the papers seem to think it's funny.'

Donna turned over the pages. 'Cor, when did everyone get so nasty? Look, this guy had been sending horrible messages to women who said they were feminists. Telling them to jump in the sea and kill themselves and things!'

The Doctor squinted. 'You're a tiny species! Why the need to constantly sub-divide?'

Donna sighed. 'I dunno. Is it Gwyneth Paltrow's fault? It usually is.'

The Doctor squinted at the paper again. He rubbed the back of his hair. 'Are they really all just having sudden heart attacks though? Young men? From too much sitting?'

'Probably,' said Donna. 'Sitting, and getting angry and raising their blood pressure and not having girlfriends.'

The Doctor frowned. 'But all of them... at their desks. Look. Two in Sydney. Four in Tokyo. One in Copenhagen... lots in San Francisco, and they all drink hemp juice and meditate out there...'

'Your nose is twitching.'

'I'm just saying. It's outwith normal human statistical bounds.'

'You think we should call the police?'

There was a pause.

'Well, you know, looking at it from a certain angle, I am *kind of* the police.'

'You're not the police!'

'I've got a box.'

'*You're not the police!*'

It was pointless. He'd already left.

'This is why I have to put so much milk in my coffee,' shouted Donna after him, standing up quickly, downing it in one, replacing the cup and running out of the door after him.

Chapter
Five

There was very little to see at the dingy apartment block belonging to Alan Tranter, the local victim, nearby in West London.

Overflowing recycling bins covered the meagre front gardens. A large woman – his neighbour – was standing outside with a sad yet slightly proud set to her jaw. She'd been interviewed by the local paper and local television, she announced to them. Then she added that obviously it was incredibly sad, obviously, and they all wanted privacy at this difficult time.

'So you knew Alan?' asked Donna.

'Not well,' said the woman, shaking her head. 'The police were round before, you know. Before he passed. They warned him to stop harassing Georgie Malone.'

'Who's that?' said the Doctor.

The woman squinted at him curiously.

Donna pulled on his coat. 'Starlet,' she hissed. 'Famous for going to premieres in not a lot of clothes.'

'*Famous?*' said the Doctor. 'That made her *famous*?'

'Stop pretending you don't read my *Heat* subscription,' said Donna.

'I… uh… OK.'

'Excuse me,' said the woman. 'Only it's chilly out here.'

'Sorry,' said the Doctor.

'Well, like I said, he'd had the police round before for harassment.' She sniffed. 'We were surprised. He wasn't a bad lad, you know, in himself. Quiet and that. Didn't have a lot of friends.'

'Figures,' said Donna.

'Donna!' said the Doctor.

'Well, it does, doesn't it? If you're all happy and loved up you're not going to spend your life trying to make other people feel bad, are you?'

The Doctor shrugged.

'But did he seem healthy?' said Donna.

'He was a big lad,' said the woman. 'Liked his food, know what I mean? Basically, the opposite of you.' She pointed at the Doctor. 'I mean, you look like you need feeding up, know what I mean?' She grinned rather suggestively for a bereaved neighbour.

The Doctor coughed in embarrassment. 'And his family?'

'Just his mum,' said the woman. 'Treated her like a skivvy, he did. She's inconsolable. So sad her baby boy's dropped dead, you know.'

Donna nodded. She supposed it didn't matter how big someone was or how inexplicable the way they behaved. They were still somebody's baby.

'We're just going to take a look at his computer,' said the Doctor. He had the psychic paper all ready, but the woman waved him on without bothering to glance at it.

'He's one of those dead trolls, innee?' she said suddenly, an oddly eager tone in her voice.

The Doctor's brow creased.

'You know,' the woman said. 'My boy. My kid. He had to change schools because people were bullying him on the internet. Sending him horrible messages, all day, all night, all over his social media, because he were a little bit different. Just for the spite of it.' She sniffed. 'Good riddance to that sort, if you ask me. And I bet a lot of people agree with me.'

And she turned round and went back into her house, closing the door forcefully behind her.

Chapter
Six

The flat had a curious emptiness about it, even though Alan had only been dead for a day; an odd, empty aura, as if the space itself knew he was gone.

A bluebottle sat on the hall windowsill. Dust lay thick on surfaces which must have been there for a long time, and there was a heavy, shut-in scent of sweat and clothes that hadn't been dried properly, and, Donna thought, sadness, but that may just have been her mood, and the circumstances in which they were there.

'What if the real police turn up while we're here?' she said to the Doctor. 'Can mine say Detective Chief Inspector on the paper? I've always wanted to say that. Hello! I'm Detective Chief Inspector Noble. 100 wpm and licensed to fingerprint.'

'Yup. If I can be the maverick copper who bends the rules and doesn't respect authority but still gets results.'

'You'd need a leather jacket.'

The Doctor winced.

Donna's grin faded as they entered the small conversion. There were three rooms on the top floor of the building; a dirty kitchen with an unsorted bin overflowing with fast-food wrappers; a sad sitting room with nothing in it but a squeaky leatherette sofa with one huge indentation in it, obviously his normal seat, and a vast television unit, and, in the bedroom, which contained a single bed with a duvet but no duvet cover, two huge computer screens and an enormous CPU, still humming.

'I thought the police would have taken this away.'

'I'm not sure the police see it as a job yet,' said the Doctor. 'At the moment it's a health issue. It isn't a crime.'

'At the moment,' came a deep voice.

The Doctor and Donna whipped around. In the doorway was the silhouette of an extremely large man. He was almost bald, just a short razored suggestion of hair dirtying his scalp. His shoulders filled the doorway. He had a long black coat on, and a pair of wraparound sunglasses gave him a completely blank expression that did not suggest that levity would be a good approach. He also wore the kind of earpiece Donna associated with FBI agents in American films.

He stepped forwards slowly. 'Seeing two strange people poking about, though. That makes it look more... interesting?'

'Nothing strange about me,' said the Doctor, as Donna shot him a look. 'What?' He strode forward. 'Hi. I'm the Doctor.'

The tall man said nothing, simply grunted. 'I'm here to remove the computer,' he said, making a move towards it.

'Are you from the police?' said Donna.

He turned to her. 'Are you?'

'Umm, kind of?'

'Well, surely you'd know, then,' said the man calmly, carrying on.

He jerked the hard drive up, pulling out all the leads carelessly, and dumped the unit into a huge evidence bag.

Donna stepped forward, an eager look on her face. 'Well, I'm Detective Chief Inspector—'

The Doctor stepped forwards and interrupted, much to Donna's annoyance. 'What are you looking for in that thing?' he said, nodding to it. 'Is it somewhere he's been? Some site he'd been visiting?'

'Not a clue,' said the man. 'Scuse me.' He looked down at Donna. 'Detective Chief Inspector.'

There was a stand-off in the room; a sudden nasty air of tension you could feel.

'Unless,' the man said suddenly, 'you'd like to come down to the station with me?'

'We would,' said the Doctor, confident, as ever, in his ability to talk his way out of practically anything.

Behind the man, Donna was suddenly shaking her head furiously.

'Or,' said the Doctor, 'we could come down and check on what you've done later. *What?*' he hissed, but Donna still kept on shaking her head.

Before he could respond, the man pushed past them, and left the room, carrying the CPU and screens as though they weighed nothing at all, and vanished down the stairs.

'Why couldn't we go down to the police station?' said the Doctor, watching behind him as the man disappeared, once again blocking the light from the stairwell as he heaved the bags outside and they prepared to follow him. 'What's your problem? We should either go...'

He watched the man leave by the front door and they stole carefully down the stairs.

'... or call his bluff. Which I reckon might be much more interesting. Do you see my cunning police instincts kicking in?'

Donna looked embarrassed and whispered something.

'What?'

Donna mumbled but the Doctor heard without a problem.

'You have unpaid *parking fines*?'

'Excuse me! Who once left the TARDIS bang slap in the middle of the Old Kent Road for a fortnight when we went to the Great Exhibition?'

'That's not the point.'

They looked at one another.

'Well, where do you think he's going, then?' said Donna.

They ran quickly down the rest of the stairs. But by the time they hit the entrance he'd vanished. There wasn't a trace of him in either direction.

Some distance away – he moved with extraordinary speed when he had to – the huge bulk of a man took off his wraparound sunglasses and blinked. His irises weren't brown or blue or hazel.

They were a dark yellow: the colour of pus.

Chapter
Seven

'Mother and child parking? *Donna*.' The Doctor's face was entirely disapproving.

'Oh come on, the amount of times they bark my ankles with their buggies, they deserve it.' She thought for a moment. 'He didn't *seem* like the police.' Something else struck her. '*And* he's got all the stuff that was on those computers.'

The Doctor held up the sonic smugly. 'Fortunately, he walked straight past me on his way out.'

'Did you get it all in that?'

'Every single bit. And I wiped the hard drive.'

Donna clapped her hands together. 'That's great!'

'Unless he really is the police, of course,' said the Doctor gloomily. 'Then we could have done with his help.'

The Doctor had read the entire contents of the computer on Donna's phone before her tea had cooled enough for her to sip it.

'What's on it?' asked Donna. 'What's it like?'

The Doctor grimaced. 'Like wading through sewage,' he said. He looked out of the window at people passing by on the pavement, many of them engrossed in their phones even as they walked into others on the street. 'What on earth is this compulsion... this desire to cause misery and shame for others in the internet?'

'It's just like throwing fruit at people in the stocks, innit?' said Donna equably. 'Not much changes.'

'But it's on such a vile scale now... attacking anything. Gender, clothing, weight...'

'It's just people who've done nothing with their lives trying to make themselves feel better by making other people feel worse.'

'How does that even work?' said the Doctor. '*Does* it work?'

'Dunno,' said Donna, who still felt on the receiving end after Hettie.

The Doctor looked down at the readout, then crossly deleted it all before handing it back to Donna. 'I don't want that filth contaminating... well...' he said, frowning. 'And now look at me, all tense and wound up.'

'That's just how it goes, isn't it?' said Donna gently. 'It's infectious, all that meanness. Tea normally helps. Do you want some more?'

'This tea is amazing. Compared to yours, which is awful,' said the Doctor. 'Or am I still infected with mean?'

'No,' said Donna. 'I make it terrible on purpose so I don't have to make the tea all the time. Worked wonders when I was a temp.'

'OK,' said the Doctor, replacing the chipped Royal Doulton cup on the table. 'So. The computer was fairly common or garden bile. But I think there's more to it – and I think our oversized friend proved it simply by showing up – than just a simple heart attack. Give me your gizmo again.'

Donna obediently handed over her old phone. The Doctor sonicked it, then pulled up a screen on it and started rapidly making dots in it with his finger.

'What are those?' said Donna.

'IP addresses. Most of them fake. But if you get in underneath them, it's where the websites originate. The dark web, and the Silk Road and the layers under the normal layers.'

'What normal layers?'

'The sites you use. There's a lot more going on below. You can peel the skin off the face of the worldwide web, Donna. And what sits underneath is very, very ugly.'

Donna blinked. She glanced around the coffee shop to make sure nobody was watching them, but everyone was happily buried in their own screens, which was fortunate, as the Doctor had raised up some green light from the phone, and a fine, 3D Earth globe was now spinning around their faces.

Tiny numbers were converting into points of light that were shooting off in all directions, bouncing from territory to territory but all converging on the miniscule spot of West London. Gradually the dancing lights started to arrange themselves, changing colour as the Doctor went down and down through the encryption layers until, finally, there was a little pinging noise, and a small dot on the globe was blinking.

'There we are!' The Doctor squinted and pulled the globe a little larger, then pointed a finger at the spot. 'Where is this?'

Donna looked blank.

The Doctor pressed more firmly with his finger and looked at her quizzically. 'Donna, this is *your home planet*.'

'Yeah, but... you know... geography class... boring?' She tailed off.

The Doctor rolled his eyes and pulled it up further. 'Well. South Korea it's called now. *Gunjaji Guk* – "Land of Scholarly Gentleman". Lovely place. *Geumgangsan*: "Land of Embroidered Rivers and Mountains". Really, it's quite fantastic.'

'And that's where that guy's internet was going through?'

The Doctor nodded. 'I've traced the other deceased's computers too. They all point there.'

'On my rubbish phone? When?'

'You are human, you know. You can be *a little* slow at stuff.'

'Now who's trolling?' Donna ran a finger around the pretty filigree of the light-pointed spinning globe.

'You think we should go there instead of tracking down that guy who took the computers?'

'If he was the police he'll be right behind us.' The Doctor paused. 'And if he wasn't... he'll be right behind us.'

Chapter
Eight

The Doctor and Donna walked thoughtfully back to the TARDIS. To their surprise, it had a canopy strung up over it and a vintage VW van painted pale blue parked up in front of it, blocking the entrance.

'What's that?' said the Doctor.

Donna frowned. 'Oh, no way. Oi! Hipsters!'

Two men with very long beards wearing collarless shirts with braces looked up defensively. 'What?'

'What are you doing?'

'It's our new artisan hand-brewed coffee experience,' said one of them. 'Would you like to try it?'

'Yes please,' said the Doctor.

'No you can't!' said Donna. 'And *you* have to get out of the way!'

'Actually we qualify as one of the government's micro startup efficiency craft businesses,' said the other, who had a handlebar moustache and an interrogative tone of voice. 'So we're fine here actually.'

'Yeah, we aim to provide the finest holistic coffee experience in West London,' said the first man again. He looked dubiously at Donna unfolding the psychic paper. 'But as a startup we're kind of exempt from red tape and health and safety and so on.'

'Yeah, we see ourselves kind of going beyond all that bureaucracy, yah?' said the other one. 'I mean, really we see coffee as more of a spiritual experience. Basically our aim is to get ourselves classified as a religion.'

Both men snickered and folded their arms.

'But that's my… police box,' said the Doctor.

'It's public property,' said one of the men. 'The council says…'

'I don't care what the council says!' said the Doctor. 'Trust me, if I don't listen to the Shadow Proclamation, I'm not very likely to take on board what Hammersmith and Fulham Local Authority have to say about it.'

'What do you do with it?' said the shorter of the two men, sniggering. He had trousers rolled up to his knees. 'Call coppers?'

The Doctor glanced at Donna, who was paying for a large paper cup of hazelnut latte. 'Donna!'

'It's triple filtered!' said Donna.

'Four fifty,' said the taller of the men.

'*Seriously?*'

'Well, how about you let me just check inside it, grab something I've left there,' said the Doctor.

'No,' said the bearded man. 'Don't mess with us. We've squatted before. Trust us, we know our rights. We let you in there, we're done for.'

'I'm not a squatter!' said the Doctor.

Donna looked at him.

'I'm not! Well... not... well. Anyway. That's my box. More or less.'

The two men folded their arms.

'I should warn you,' said the taller. 'My Taekkyeon teacher says I'm profoundly gifted.' He bent out his elbows and kicked off his shoes.

The Doctor grinned. 'Does he now?'

Donna glanced around. Something strange was happening. A crowd had gathered. And they were all filming on their phones. 'Doctor...' she said.

'What? Come on, I want to see this guy do some Taekkyeon. In those trousers. It'll be hilarious!'

'No, Doctor. Look. They're all filming you.'

The Doctor spun round. 'Why?'

'In case you have a fight or something. Then they'll upload it on the internet.'

'What? *Why?*'

Donna shrugged. 'That's just what people do now.'

The bystanders looked eager, hungry, unpleasant smiles on their faces.

Except one, the Doctor noticed. One, a young woman, was touching, suddenly, at her chest, as if she'd felt something there.

'Are you all right?' he said to her.

'Get out of my space,' she spat back at him, still holding up the phone.

The Doctor took a step back and glanced at Donna. 'Actually,' he said 'It might make sense to trace the route physically. Get a sense for what's actually going on on the ground. Good instincts. Good police work.'

'Do you mean run away?' said Donna.

'A temporary retreat…'

'Actually,' said Donna, hailing a cab. ' It *is* pretty good coffee. And you know what: if we're going somewhere on Earth, I think a trip sounds like fun. Who needs the TARDIS? Let's take a trip!'

Chapter
Nine

'Why would a coffee shop owner want to attack me with violence, though? It doesn't make sense,' said the Doctor as they went through Heathrow.

Donna looked with pleasure at the short security line and the departures board indicating hundreds of fascinating locations. 'Modern life doesn't make sense,' she said. 'Anyway, I'm enjoying myself. I've always wanted to go travelling.'

The Doctor gave her a very hard stare at that.

'Excuse me,' the security woman was saying to him.

The Doctor turned his full high-beam grin on her, but it didn't appear to be having the usual effect.

'This can't go through hand baggage. You'll need to check it in, or we can dispose of it for you.'

The Doctor looked at her in horror. 'But it's... I mean... It's just a screwdriver.'

'No screwdrivers,' said the woman in a bored voice pointing to a set of guidelines on the wall. 'No guns, knives, liquids, needles, exotic animals, or—'

'Screwdrivers,' said the Doctor reluctantly.

Donna wasn't listening. She'd got past security, and was now being directed by a handsome young steward to the lounge.

The Doctor relinquished his screwdriver to the baggage hold with no little anguish, and followed Donna through to the softly lit carpeted luxury of the first-class lounge.

Donna was standing in the middle of it, being noisy.

'You mean we could have been travelling like this *all this time*? I spent all that time in that *box thing* when I could have been—'

'Would you like some champagne, madam?' interrupted the handsome steward.

'Yes please.' Donna thrust her arm out and the man put a glass in it with a smile.

'Seriously! All this time!'

The Doctor looked wounded. 'You truly prefer this to the TARDIS?'

The man coughed and leaned forwards again. 'Would you like some complimentary pyjamas, madam? For sleeping on the flight? And perhaps a massage?'

'Yes to the pyjamas, no to the massage. Can't trust 'em,' said Donna steadily, still staring at the Doctor. 'Where are my TARDIS pyjamas, eh?'

'You're seriously telling me you prefer moving around a single planet at a snail's pace to my beautiful ship?'

Donna was looking down the expansive menu. 'Caviar? Hmm. Foie gras? No, that's cruel.'

'We can make you anything you like, madam,' said the steward.

'I would really like a toasted cheese sandwich,' said Donna. 'With extra marmite. Want anything?'

The Doctor shook his head.

'Certainly madam.' And the steward melted away.

'Seriously? You really prefer this?'

They were in the air now, and the Doctor was still going on.

'Shut up,' said Donna, putting the soft-lined eye mask up over her hair in preparation for later, and smothering the expensive face cream they'd given her all over herself.

The Doctor was half-lying, half-sitting on top of the flat bed seat at the pointy end of the plane, looking extremely bored and uncomfortable.

'Aren't you enjoying it?' asked Donna.

'People keep asking if they can get me stuff. And I say, "Can you get me my screwdriver?" and they say, "No."'

'Ssh,' said Donna. 'I have seventeen episodes of *The Apprentice* to catch up on. Everyone in it is particularly awful and unlikeable this year.'

The Doctor frowned. 'More contempt served up as mass entertainment. I don't get it.'

'Well, Alan Sugar, right…'

'No, I mean. All of it. Hate as a way to communicate. It's new.'

He disappeared and reappeared two minutes later.

'Where'd you go?'

The Doctor showed off his screwdriver, looking marginally more cheerful. 'You know they've got a little lift?' he said. 'It's awesome. I love a little lift.'

His attention was taken, suddenly, by a large man a few rows behind. He looked the epitome of business-like, sober responsibility, in his expensive suit and silk socks. But in the lounge the Doctor had noticed him, hitting his keys furiously; complaining loudly to staff about the slowness of the internet connection. The frustration boiled off him, as clearly as if you could see little wavy lines emanating from his head.

He'd noticed something else too. The Doctor almost never felt the cold. But he'd noticed a cold corner of air where the businessman was, even though the man was sweating angrily. Just as he'd noticed a cold spot in the room in Alan's house. It was strange.

There was a terrible, slow internet connection available on the aeroplane itself, although few of the passengers were paying attention to it. Most of them were sleeping or watching films, or eating or, if they were Donna, attempting to do all three things at once.

The Doctor paced up and down. Whenever Donna raised an annoyed eyebrow at him, he pretended to be doing the stretching exercises that came with the welcome pack, which earned him a suspicious look.

He hovered next to the man. 'Having trouble getting online?' he said sympathetically. 'Me too.'

'This airline sucks,' said the man.

'It's not the best way of getting places,' said the Doctor encouragingly. 'Are you trying to get some work done?'

'Yeah' said the man. 'I have a bunch of total putzes to fire, and I can't get the thing fired up?'

'You fire them over an email.'

'Yeah,' said the man. 'Stops them getting all worked up.'

'Does it really?' The Doctor glanced around. 'Does it feel cold to you in here?'

The man looked up. 'Yeah,' he said. Useless bloody airline, they can't get anything right. Complete waste of everyone's time. Load of useless chancers.'

The Doctor nodded slowly. 'Do you think.'

The man smiled. 'In fact, I think I'm going to just send them a little message right now.' He typed furiously and managed to pull up a review site. 'I'll throw in a few words about the stewardesses... not exactly the lookers, are they? What do they think they pay for up here – am I right? Am I?'

The man nudged the Doctor, who closed his eyes briefly in horror. One of these days, he thought, he was going back to being a potter.

The man continued typing furiously. The Doctor watched over his shoulder. There was a stream of expletives and nasty sarcasm, copied to the airline's twitter account and any email address the man could find on their website.

Then, something happened. The temperature dropped again.

The man turned his head. 'Did you feel that?'

The Doctor nodded.

The man stared at the porthole window on his left side. 'From there – didn't you feel it? Is there a draft in here? *Stewardess!*' the man screeched loudly. 'Get me another whisky. For God's sake, does nobody do their jobs around here?'

He rattled his glass rudely at the young woman who hurried up to fulfil his demand. She scuttled off, clearly hating him; the chain of bad manners spreading ever onwards.

'And what's that draft?' he demanded, red in the face, as she returned. 'Where's that draft coming from? Is there something wrong with the plane?'

He said this at a loud enough volume for several people seated nearby to turn round.

'What does he mean, something wrong with the plane?' came a worried voice from further up the cabin.

'There's nothing wrong with the plane,' said the young stewardess, whose name badge read Amina, bravely. 'I can't feel what you're feeling, sir.'

The man's face grew even more brick red. 'Damn it, of course you'd say that. You're paid to say that. Doesn't mean anything.' He unbuckled his seatbelt.

'Could you stay in your seat, sir?' said the stewardess.

'The light isn't on,' said the man. 'I've paid for this seat. I can do what I bloody well like.'

The Doctor had been intently interested to see where the man thought the draft was coming from, but even he couldn't stand for that.

'Actually, I think the lady asked you to stay seated,' he said, as the man heaved himself up.

'Actually, I don't give a monkey's what the lady said, you big long streak of—'

The Doctor ducked in perfect time as the man, who seemed disorientated, attempted a swing at him that went slightly wrong. The man lurched into the gangway. Someone let out a startled yell.

'There's something wrong with this plane,' the man shouted incoherently. 'It's freezing! They're letting the air out! Someone's not telling us something! Something's gone wrong! Can't you feel it? What's going on out there?'

He banged hard on the window. Someone else yelled at him to stop. The Doctor glanced at Donna, but she had her headphones on and was fully engrossed in two people shouting at each other at a fancy dress party. He whipped out the sonic and tuned it in to the frequency of the window. There were cold patches and warm patches. It didn't make sense.

He frowned. The man saw him do it.

'*You* know!' he shouted menacingly. 'You know something's happening! You know!' He advanced on the Doctor. 'Tell me what it is! Tell me! I need to know! You have to tell me.'

'I'm sure it's nothing to worry about,' said the Doctor, lying through his teeth. He was, in fact, extremely worried.

Amina the stewardess ran up. 'Why don't you just retake your seat sir, and, um… We'll have a choice of chicken or fish along in a moment…'

The man cannonballed himself into the Doctor with unlikely aggression. The Doctor could feel his pulse. It was racing. He looked at him curiously.

'Are you all right?'

The man's face was now inches away from his, pressing him against the wall of the cabin. There were people screaming now and a sense of panic throughout the cabin. The man put his arm up to try and choke the Doctor.

'*Tell me what's happening out there!*' he screeched, spittle hitting the Doctor's face.

'Only, your skin feels clammy,' said the Doctor. 'And you're very, very red. Seriously, if I was your doctor…' He put his hand on the man's pulse. The man's wrist was starting to squeeze on his neck. 'Yes,' he said. 'You see, this, your pulse is completely galloping. It's very, very bad. I really think you should sit down with your head between your legs for a moment.'

The man was screaming, as were several passengers. Behind, unnoticed to anyone, the man's laptop was blinking.

'*Stop babbling and tell me what the hell's going on!*'

There was a vein now pulsing in the man's temple. The man kept up his pressure on the Doctor's windpipe, whilst drawing back his other hand to punch him in the face.

'What are you feeling?' said the Doctor, urgently.

The man blinked at that. He paused for just a second, drew a ragged breath.

'Well…' he began.

ZZAP.

The man lay stretched out on the floor. Behind him was Amina the stewardess, holding up a Taser.

'Ooh,' she said. 'I've never had to use that before.'

The Doctor blinked in annoyance. 'I was actually doing just fine.'

'You were being strangled and about to be punched in the face. It seemed the right thing to do.' Amina looked nervous for a second. 'At least, that's what it says in the manual.'

'No, no, I suppose you were absolutely right, if it's in the manual,' said the Doctor, recovering himself as the other passengers gave her a round of applause. Except for Donna, who still had her headphones on and was eating an ice cream.

The cockpit door opened and one of the pilots came out to see what the commotion was about.

On the floor, the man was stirring, and starting to struggle. Amina had brought out a pair of restraining cuffs.

'It's amazing what you guys fly with,' said the Doctor.

'Isn't it!' she replied.

'What's the deal?' said the co-pilot coming forward. 'Do we have to turn back? I'd really rather not.'

They looked at the man, who was lying and grunting on the floor

'He'll either have to deal with British police or Korean police,' said the pilot. 'Wonder if he's got a preference.'

'He's Swiss,' said Amina, checking the manifest. 'So no extradition either way. I doubt he'll care.'

The Doctor shook his head. 'I don't think this was a crime,' he said. 'I think this was a medical episode.'

Amina sniffed. 'Well, it looked a lot like a crime to me…'

'No, I think he's basically harmless and—'

What happened next happened very quickly indeed. There was a quick scrabbling noise and, with an unlikely and extraordinary strength, the man on the floor shot up and pulled down the co-pilot, grabbing his ankles with his hands until he fell down, knocking himself out on one of the large plastic seats.

Then the man shot incredibly fast through the open cockpit door and, before anyone had a chance to react, slammed the door shut behind him.

There came a muffled yell and some noise from the front of the plane – presumably as he knocked out the other pilot – and, mere moments after that, the huge airliner went into a sharp dive.

The entire thing had taken less than thirty seconds.

Chapter
Ten

Many of the occupants of the plane started to scream as the tight temporary social contract people had with one another, balanced above the world in a little tin box, dissolved and people's true panic proved very close to the surface.

The co-pilot was lying concussed on the floor. Amina swore mightily, and ran to the cockpit door, hammering to be let in.

The intercom came on over the entire plane.

The man now sounded beyond rage and into a place far, far beyond.

'I'll show you!' he said. But he didn't explain any more than this. *'I'll show you!'* he repeated. But he didn't explain who he wanted to show things to, or why.

The plane dipped some more and the warning sirens came on, along with a clear electronic voice from the cockpit saying, 'Pull up! Pull up!'

Donna finally looked up, then whipped her head round to find the Doctor, shocked. She fumbled with her seatbelt and moved towards him. 'What's happening? Fix it!'

The Doctor was looking thoughtfully out of the window, as the plane continued to plummet towards the ground.

The sound it made – not just the alarm, but the push of metal diving at an angle it was not meant to experience, the G-forces straining against it – was almost intolerable. Not to mention the screaming.

Donna bustled towards him, looking out over the panicking rows of people. 'Um, excuse me? Want to get a move on? Lots of people's worst nightmare happening here?' She turned to them. 'Everyone stay in your seats!' she said in what was meant to be a reassuring voice. 'It'll be fine! Don't worry, we'll fix this. Don't worry.'

Out of the window, the lights of Asia down below were shining and tilting as the plane bumped massively downwards through the atmosphere in a great sweeping whoosh; like a bone through skin, the horrible sense of a world gone horribly, sickeningly wrong.

Things started to fall and drop upwards; shoes, bags, glasses; knives and forks. Someone hit their arm and started to sob in low tones that cut through the screams.

Everyone on the plane was in a state of total panic; except for one passenger in a seat near the back; a large man, who had not taken his sunglasses off for the entire flight. He nested his head on the inflight pillow, and casually dropped off to sleep.

*

'Any time you like, please, Doctor?' said Donna, trying not to let a note of impatience creep into her voice. 'Yeah, all right,' she said to a smart-suited businessman who was weeping.

He reached over, grabbed her hand and muttered something.

She snatched back her hand. 'No, I'm not kissing you! You can kiss your wife with gratitude when you get home, thanks! Don't worry, it'll be fine… Doctor!'

'I think… I think I have it,' the Doctor was saying, still looking out the window. 'I think I know…. it's in the back of my mind… I've seen this… I've seen it. But it gets eaten up, until you think it's simply rage, or fury, a passing mood that burns itself out… but sometimes it isn't… Let me talk to him.'

'What, the madman that's trying to crash us into a mountain?' said Donna. 'Hey, I have an idea: save us all first, talk afterwards, right.'

'He won't know afterwards,' said the Doctor grimly.

The stewardess was walking up the aisle, making sure everyone had their seatbelts on and telling people to brace.

'Amina, what's his name?'

'Kenneth Phillips,' said Amina shortly, carrying on.

'Cor, you're a good stewardess,' said the Doctor, watching her head down the aisle. 'Look at you! All helpful and brilliant!'

Amina turned back, her eyes betraying her fear. 'Please take your seat, sir,' she said, with a tremble in her voice.

With a BANG all the oxygen masks descended at the same moment. There was more sobbing. Lots of people were scribbling notes, or trying to record themselves on their mobile phones. One person was screaming repeatedly. Amina went to comfort them.

'I mean, you're exactly the type of person we need,' said the Doctor, looking after her, holding on to the seat back to stop himself toppling down the steep incline. 'Very impressed.'

Donna folded her arms. 'Fine,' she said in exasperation. 'I'll do it.'

And she whipped his sonic screwdriver out of his pocket and hauled herself hand over hand on the seat backs down to the front of the plane.

'Hey!' shouted the Doctor. 'Hey! Don't do that! Don't ever do that! Don't touch my... Don't go near my... It's my...'

Donna had got the door open by the time the Doctor caught her up. She whipped round to face him.

'There's terrified children back there,' she said in a low voice. 'Fix this now and figure out the other thing later.'

The Doctor looked at her sternly. He was, she realised, genuinely cross, and she meekly handed over the screwdriver.

'You don't get it Donna,' he said in a low voice. 'If I don't figure this out now, there won't be any later.'

Chapter
Eleven

Inside the cockpit, Kenneth Phillips was leaning over the steering bar. He was still conscious and had it pulled up to its absolute maximum, so the plane was plummeting. He was muttering to himself.

'I'll show them! I'll show them all!'

Somehow, seeing land approaching from the front of the plane – and the nose of the aircraft was nearly directly pointed at the ground now – was far more frightening than seeing it from the side porthole, where you could almost believe that it was disconnected and they weren't all plunging to their deaths. Donna gulped.

The Doctor barely glanced outside, simply leaned casually against the pilot's seat to steady himself. A red light was blinking alarmingly and the alarms were at a high pitch.

'Hello, Kenneth. Ken? Kenny? You don't look like a Kenny. I like Kennys. They have a tendency to play the accordion. You don't—'

'Get away from me. You can't stop me. You can't.'

'Right, Kenneth. I see.'

'You can't calm me down.'

Kenneth turned his red-rimmed eyes on the Doctor. He was completely deranged, way beyond the normal bounds of fury; he seemed to be in a place far, far away.

'I'll show you,' he spat. 'I'll show you all.'

'What can you feel, Kenneth?'

'I feel furious! I've been mistreated and bullied and disrespected for long enough.'

'No, no Kenneth. I'm not asking *how* you feel. I can see how you feel. That's fine. I need to know *what* you feel.'

The alarms were getting deafening now. 'PULL UP PULL UP' was sounding, and the red alarm was flashing round and round.

Amina entered, and shut the cockpit door behind them. Her face was furious. 'Straighten up the plane,' she said, holding the Taser out in front of her like a weapon. *'Straighten us up!'*

'In a minute,' said the Doctor, waving the Taser away and tutting. 'I need a minute.' He moved closer to Kenneth's ear. 'What are you feeling, Kenneth? What can you feel? Tell me.'

Kenneth's mouth moved in his brick-red face, but no sound came out; he was so horrified by the enormity of what was happening as the huge jet continued to cascade downwards. The noise was unbelievable.

Donna suddenly felt properly frightened. Normally when she was in a confined space with the

Doctor, she felt safe. This was different. He didn't seem to have the faintest interest in sorting them out. Below them she could make out plains and towns and mountains. She found herself hoping it would be a mountain, avoid a populated area. Her hands were trembling.

'Straighten up…'

'Could you… just for a moment. Donna. Can you hold her?' said the Doctor.

Donna grabbed Amina's arm. 'Sorry about this, but can you be quiet?

'But we can be saved!' Amina's eyes were wide as Donna clapped a hand over her mouth.

'I am so sorry about this,' said Donna. 'I really am. We kind of have to do this kind of trust-y thing. I'm no happier about it than you are. Hurry up, Doctor!'

There was a bang. Amina started and muttered something under Donna's hand.

'Engine gone?' said Donna.

Amina nodded.

Donna started to bounce up and down.

'*Move yourself!*' she yelled at the Doctor. In doing so, she lost her footing briefly as the plane lurched, and Amina took the opportunity to push her hand away and break free of Donna's grip.

Immediately there was a huge zapping noise.

'Aha!' said the Doctor. 'Stop it! That tickles!'

Amina zapped him again, and he giggled. 'Argh, stop! Please. There's no time. Stop! Hahaha! *Argh!*'

He writhed uncontrollably as Donna tried to grab the Taser from Amina.

Now they could make out topographical features on the ground: fields, plains, a mountain. A mountain right below them.

The hubbub beyond the doors continued; now there were people banging at the door, men's voices shouting out in desperation to let them in, for heaven's sake; it wasn't too late, it wasn't too late, let them in…

'A finger,' came a voice, suddenly, almost too quiet to be heard over the noise of everything else that was going on, as the alarms beeped and Donna stared out of the window into the abyss, the unbelievable way the great machine was approaching the earth; the very end… in a plummeting jet…

For a fraction of a second nobody moved. Then the Doctor crouched down, still twitching a little.

Kenneth had spoken.

'What?' the Doctor said. 'Say that again.'

'A finger. Icy fingers,' said Kenneth, as spittle came out of his mouth. 'Argh… Oh… It hurts… It's twisting… The finger is twisting.'

The Doctor started nodding, frantically, as the man contorted and his limbs lurched out, then coiled back in on himself again, breathless, unable to speak with the pain; his face no longer red, but the palest, bloodless white. He glanced up at the girls. 'Take him!'

And as Donna and Amina pulled the now unconscious man from his seat, he slipped into it.

The nose of the plane was almost fully tilted towards the ground. Donna could see the rocks on the mountain; the grey stone tipped with snow almost entirely and she couldn't help it; she would normally have said that she trusted the Doctor 100 per cent. But now she felt it was possibly 99.99999 per cent. She closed her eyes and opened her mouth to scream as the rock filled the air and the window grew dark and the Doctor grabbed the controls...

Donna's stomach lurched as the Doctor pulled the throttle full back, and she lost her footing again as the plane abruptly turned upwards. She could hear Amina clearly repeating: 'Don't stall don't stall don't stall don't stall...'

Donna crouched down, and she and Amina threw themselves into trying to resuscitate Kenneth, who was lying on the floor, completely unconscious.

They banked steeply, and finally, gradually, the aeroplane ascended above the clouds and straightened out.

The Doctor turned round. 'Can you hold the plane?' he said to Amina.

'I can try,' she said.

'Get back!' the Doctor shouted at Donna, as he leapt off the chair and down to where Kenneth was lying. He grabbed the first aid box and found some adrenaline. He plunged it into the man's heart, but it had no effect.

He tried again and again, but nothing, and when Donna finally looked away she realised that the co-pilot had recovered. They were once more taking on a smooth route, and if it weren't for the red alarms still flashing and the noisy commotion coming from air traffic control, you might think nothing had happened at all.

Donna looked down at Kenneth again. His face had gone completely slack and blue; the blood was draining now; everything had left his body.

'More adrenaline,' said the Doctor. He was still palpitating the man's chest, but it was becoming increasingly apparent that it was no use.

'Doctor.'

He couldn't bear it, she knew. He couldn't bear to lose even one single tiny prospect of life. The tiniest spark; the meagrest hope.

But Kenneth was plainly dead. Behind the Doctor, the onboard computer whirred and beeped. Everyone ignored it.

Eventually the Doctor sat back on his heels, looking down at Kenneth.

'He nearly killed us all,' said Donna, gently.

'That's not how it works,' said the Doctor, his mouth a firm line.

Amina was leaving the cockpit. The Doctor stood up and turned to her.

'You were totally fantastic by the way,' he said to the girl, who was still trembling a little. 'I mean, really amazing. And so *useful*!'

Donna folded her arms. It struck home. She knew he didn't mean it that way, but he was making her feel a bit like Hettie had. And she didn't like it. 'I was useful!'

'I mean… you can just do so much… fly a plane… prepare an injection… keep passengers calm… Taser people at the wrong moment…and I bet you've never stolen someone's sonic screwdriver.'

Amina flushed. 'Just part of the service…'

'Yeah, if we'd been in economy class she'd probably just have left us,' said Donna, but nobody was listening to her.

Chapter
Twelve

The plane managed to limp into Seoul's Incheon Airport, even with an engine missing. The traumatised passengers had to wait as officials came on board and hustled off all of those involved with the incident, including the Doctor and Donna.

'We just saw it happen,' Donna explained loudly to a policeman, who stopped and looked at her. He blinked. The next thing they knew they were locked up in a room.

'Why? Why are they locking us up?' Donna asked them and the Doctor, who smiled wryly.

'What?'

'You'll see.'

The next thing, several uniformed men marched in: a mixture, clearly, of police and army. They fired questions at Donna, who answered as honestly as she could without arousing suspicions by mentioning blue boxes or anything else.

'What's going on?' she said eventually 'What? Why do they keep laughing at me?'

The Doctor was leaning against the wall not paying attention. 'Oh yeah,' he said. 'Yeah, they think you're a spy…'

'What? Why? Me? You know, I've always thought I would make an awesome spy. But why do they think… Oh.' She realised.

'Because your Korean is so good.'

Donna smiled at them. 'Oh, how kind of you to say! Thank you!'

The man nodded back, then burst out laughing again.

'I have pointed out to him that there aren't very many red-haired spies in Korea,' the Doctor went on.

'Me and my perfect Korean!' said Donna, ignoring him, and marvelling at herself. She felt the shape her mouth moved as she spoke.

'You know it's not you doing it,' said the Doctor.

'Shut up,' said Donna. 'It's nice to feel accomplished. Ooh, I was looking for a phrase to say I'm feeling proud of myself, but I can't find one. How strange. Korean is really different from English.'

The Doctor gave her a funny look.

'What?'

'What would ever make you think you weren't accomplished?'

'You! On the plane! With Miss Perfect Stewardess who's great at everything. So maybe you should travel with her, seeing as she's so great at everything.'

The Doctor frowned. 'Why would I want to travel with someone who's great at everything? That would make me look absolutely awful.'

Donna gave him a look.

'You're free to go,' said one of the uniformed men.

'In a minute,' said Donna. 'If you hadn't noticed, we're about to have a fight?'

They were quickly ushered out through the terminal doors.

By the time they hit the city it was lunchtime.

It was a beautiful day, sunny and warm, and the strangeness of the street food vendors and the sleek cars and the high glass buildings were all novelty to Donna. She was enjoying it all hugely, especially the luxury of being able to speak to people. But she was still cross with the Doctor and didn't want him to see her having a good time.

'So aren't you going to ask me what's happening?' said the Doctor eventually, as they crossed the great Gwanghwamun Square, with its statues and memorials, and high hotels and offices all around.

The Doctor would have been embarrassed to admit, given the obvious prosperity of its contemporary citizens, that he had slightly preferred Seoul in the Silla dynasty, and had fond memories of its perfumed fountains and pleasure gardens. He found the constant pushing up of buildings towards the heavens generally an unnerving development.

'No,' said Donna. 'I'm going to eat whatever that is…' She walked towards a vendor and picked some up. 'What is this?'

'*Bundegi*.'

It took Donna a moment.

'Umm. Excellent. Deep-fried silk larvae.'

She walked on, chewing with some difficulty, but again determined not to let him notice she'd made a mistake.

'Well the thing is—'

'I mean, I'm sure Amina would be a really good listener.'

'Are you going to keep this up? Because we don't have much time. Are those good?'

'Want some?'

'No, you're all right...'

'I always get hungry after I've been in a plane crash,' said Donna. She turned to face him finally. 'What was it then? That made you make us wait *so long*?'

'That made you steal my screwdriver?'

The traffic honked on the incredibly crowded crossing. They strode across, standing out, cross with one another.

'Well. It was...' The Doctor sighed as he looked for the right way to explain it. 'Well. They were... I think. You have an infestation.'

'Me?' Donna looked dubiously at the silkworms.

'The planet.'

'Oh,' she said. 'I'm not sure I'm hungry any more.'

They walked on, round the extraordinary glittering metal city hall.

'What kind of an infestation?'

'It's a parasite. In the blood. From the Rafirax system, generally. You can never take your dog in. Quarantine is thirty years. Wonder how it got here?'

'What does it do? Is that what that guy in the plane had?'

'Yes. But I had to find out from him. It has a tricky diagnostic pathology, because it looks like you're having a heart attack, or a fit. But no. They're called Rempaths. They're tiny organisms, transported through blood. But they're actually transmitted through… well through the internet, here. They travel through technology, looking for living hosts.'

'Ugh,' said Donna.

'Then they feed off… well, they feed off emotional energy I suppose. Specifically, anger. Anger produces hormones which they feed on. And they turn that on itself, spawning and respawning and performing a kind of furious feedback loop in the host…'

'Why do they kill you, then?' said Donna.

'Lots of parasites kill the host,' said the Doctor. 'Usually when there's enough of them to burst out and feed back into the network… it's why you spit when you're angry.'

'I don't spit when I'm angry!'

'It's why every mammal in the galaxy spits when they're angry except for you.' The Doctor rubbed his neck. 'And who are the angriest people in the world?'

'Terrorists?' hazarded Donna.

The Doctor shook his head, sadly. 'No. All of their anger is out, I'm afraid; in the air around us.' He sighed. 'No. No. It strikes people who are frustrated but generally can't do anything about it. Who are stuck. So the Rempaths circulate and build up and build up.'

'Your classic internet troll,' said Donna. 'In front of his computer, typing angrily about stuff he can't do anything about.'

'He?' said the Doctor.

'Oh yeah,' said Donna, realising. 'No, my friend Hettie, she gets right antsy about women who do children differently from her... She's always on the internet telling them off about it... Oh my God. You don't think she might be...'

The Doctor blinked. 'That friend you were staying with?'

'She got the right hump with me!'

'Who could possibly do that?'

'Shut up... Oh goodness, Doctor, is it fixable?'

The Doctor paused for a long time.

'That bad?' said Donna gently.

'It can be. When people start to die, other people start to get upset and angry and go online to complain about it and... well, you can see.'

'What's it feel like?'

'According to the literature, it feels like an icy finger, reaching out. Reaching out to grasp at your heart. To turn it to a shard of ice.'

Donna blinked. 'Like the Snow Queen?'

The Doctor nodded. 'Yes. It's quite the historical document.'

Donna looked around. Everywhere on the bustling streets people were staring down at their phones. Tapping, typing. Nearly walking into others, and tutting crossly when they did so.

'Remember,' said the Doctor. 'Rempaths need two things to proliferate: a connection… and anger.'

Donna shivered. It was such a beautiful day. But now around her she couldn't help thinking… She looked at a man standing on a street corner, shouting into his phone about his car service not turning up in time… And the woman over there, what was making her so upset that she was reading… Would these people… The idea of people gradually getting angrier and angrier, until they died and continued the cycle…

Would humanity give up its devices if they were warned what was coming?

'We're doomed,' said Donna. She looked at him. He was nodding.

'It is very difficult that the nature of the disease is precisely what would make you not listen to someone telling you how to not get the disease.'

'So, why did it start here?'

'Fastest, best internet in the world. Everything starts here. Including the horrible ones.'

They were standing in front of a row of cafés, all of which were set up like computer labs, with juice bars at one end and rows and rows of large screens in front of them. Young lads were sitting, gaming furiously, typing, throwing things at each other, drinking and teasing one another. It looked like a school where the teacher had left the room.

'Hang on,' said Donna, as they crossed the road towards it. 'Does this mean I'm going to have to be, like, all lovely and nice all the time in case I get the disease?'

The Doctor looked at her. 'Why don't you just be lovely and nice all the time because that's the right thing to do?' he said.

'Because, Spaceboy,' said Donna, 'not all of us have billion-square-foot mansions that can fly to live in. And no job. Or bills. Or mortgage. Or annoying families to worry about.'

The Doctor turned to look at her quizzically. 'Seriously?'

'You don't even have an alarm clock!'

'I… I do so have an alarm clock!'

'Yes, which you used to time that skipping race we had.'

'I still think you—'

'I did *not* make an illegal move! There are no illegal moves in skipping!'

'I'm just saying—'

'Noillegalemovesinskipping' said Donna quickly as she stepped back onto the pavement.

The Doctor raked his fingers through his hair in agitation. 'Do you really… Do you really think I have an absolutely amazing life with nothing to get worried about?'

Donna straightened up and looked at him. 'Well, if you can't, who can?' she said gently. And then, still seeing no reaction, 'So, why don't we just pretend that you do?'

And they disappeared into the bustling crowds of the city.

Chapter
Thirteen

The noise levels of the shoot-em-up games and Skype conversations inside the cafés was immense.

Everywhere they went, the Doctor went behind the scenes and started up a conversation about routers and hp speed that Donna couldn't follow at all, so she went and watched the kids play.

They were playing military games for the most part: running joint missions and blowing other people up with astonishing skill and alacrity. She watched them quietly, even as they looked at her with nervous curiosity, and she saw the teenagers they truly were behind their eyes. Just boys after all. Even if their gaming machine guns looked eerily like the real thing. Even with the noise and the shouting. The jump from that to actual shooting, with excitable, hysterical teenage boys, and...

She was lost in thought as the Doctor re-emerged from the latest place they'd visited, folding a napkin into his pocket. The café owner looked furtive and grave, and watched them thoughtfully as they left the building.

'What did you say to him?' said Donna glancing behind her. 'He looks very unhappy.'

'I'm not sure,' said the Doctor. 'The psychic paper came up with something that said *Gukga anjeon bowibu*, and that pretty much did it.'

'So, where are we going?'

'Aha,' said the Doctor. 'He knew exactly what we were after. And he didn't even care why.' His face was sad for a second. 'OK. The fastest, darkest most secret side of the web… Hey!'

He hailed a little motor scooter that was passing, which had a double seat mounted on the back of it. The traffic on Seoul's wide streets was alarming, but this seemed designed to whip through it, however precariously.

'This is more like it.' The Doctor sat back cheerfully as the little bike puttered speedily through horrifyingly slender gaps in the incredibly dense traffic. Hundreds of cyclists had to veer out of their way as they tore towards them, the driver shouting cheerful abuse all the while, and getting some back. Donna shut her eyes.

'You're the one who wanted to travel in a different way!' said the Doctor.

'Yes, in luxury, not as a near-death experience!'

The Doctor laughed as they narrowly missed a huge old open truck full of goats. 'Come on, live a little.'

'A very little,' said Donna. 'Does he know where he's going?'

No sooner had she said this than the little vehicle crossed the astonishing Banpo bridge, with its coloured fountain of water cascading down, into the older town of Yongsang, where it soon turned off and darted down a narrow, practically invisible side street.

Instantly things changed. After the shiny cars and huge skyscrapers of Gangnam, here there were narrow alleyways and closely built apartments teetering towards each other; washing hanging in between the windows on ropes. Stray dogs darted past them and they splashed through puddles that looked as though they had been there for some time.

'Uh oh,' said Donna. 'Now I'm getting a bit anxious and foreign about this.'

'Ssh,' said the Doctor. 'He knows where we mean.'

And the bike swung round into a little cobbled square. They were deep in what was left of Seoul's old town by now; a wooden temple sat there, its low doors swinging open. The houses were sometimes little more than brightly coloured shacks, slightly listing.

Here there were bolder stone buildings, with pagoda built roofs, and glimpses of the old city walls. It was rather charming. Everywhere people went about their business, not in the sharp suits and western fashions of the main streets, but, once or twice Donna saw, in more traditional dress. Children's voices rang out, as well as many more little scooters honking their way through lanes far too narrow for cars.

Finally, tucked away behind a square in Itaewon, there was a tiny alleyway. Four restaurants stood in a row. None of them appeared to sell anything other than pig's feet.

'I'm not sure I'm in the mood,' frowned Donna as she paid the man and the Doctor strode off behind one of the ornate little wooden huts. The building was half stone – at the bottom – and half wood, with the now familiar pagoda-style tilted roof. Tiling was inlaid into the walls, with complex figures carved on them Donna couldn't decipher. They glanced at each other.

Then they pushed open the heavy red wooden door and entered in.

The room beyond did not have to go silent; it was already silent.

It was huge, far larger than it looked from the outside. Immaculately clean and quiet, with a steel door facing them and, to their right, banks of computers, brand new and sleek. Their large screens hummed quietly. Behind each one was a man or a woman, an international mix, each fiercely concentrating, their eyes flickering nervously upwards as the Doctor and Donna entered but then straight down again and away. There was a deeply hushed feeling in the room, like the reading room at the British Library, or an operating theatre: a sense of fierce embedded concentration. Nobody spoke.

'Morning!' said the Doctor, sizing up the room in an instant. 'Now, somebody must know which of those four pig's feet restaurants is the best. I love the artisan quarter, don't you?'

A large local man who had been standing silently behind the door stepped forward. He towered over both of them. 'I think you are in the wrong place,' he said gravely.

'Now that,' said the Doctor to Donna. 'Him saying that basically proves that he's in the right place. Totally!'

'Totally,' agreed Donna.

'And you must leave,' said the man. He looked briefly to his side. A rather furious-looking curved sword was tucked into his belt.

'Ooh,' said Donna. 'That's really lovely. I mean, that's a proper big sword that is. I mean, you could easily take off two, three heads at a time with that. Easy.'

The man frowned, and drew the sword. All the faces at screens behind them, amazingly, simply bowed down and went back to work, as if they weren't there. If anything bad was going to happen, Donna realised, they weren't going to be helped or saved by a single person in this room. Which pretty much solved the problem of whether what they were up to was good or not.

Not.

'You distract him and I'll do some sword kicking,' she whispered to the Doctor.

'Sword kicking?' said the Doctor 'Honestly, I don't think that's a thing.'

'It might be a thing,' said Donna, swinging her ankle. 'You don't know that.'

'I'm sure they teach them how to fend off sword kickers,' said the Doctor. 'Seriously, that's, like, day two.'

'You. Finger,' the man grunted at Donna.

'You what?'

Without ceremony, the man grabbed her hand, slammed it down on the desk, and separated out her pinkie. Then he lifted his sword.

'One finger per minute. Until you leave.'

Donna squealed. 'Not that one! I wear my nan's ring on it!'

The Doctor gently put his arm between the sword and Donna's hand. 'Go for this one,' he said. 'I've got a spare.'

The man blinked in confusion.

'But before you do, you may want to mention to whoever is behind that door…' He raised his head to the security cameras and gave them a wide and cheerful grin. 'Hey! Person! On the other side of the door! You know that there's Rempaths on the loose? They've been unleashed on Earth and they're moving through the internet? You may not know what they are, in which case I strongly recommend we stop and chat. But if you *do* know what they are, then… well, I don't know how you feel about the widespread potential loss of your client base. It seems to me something you might like to discuss. Because I might be able to stop it.'

The man drew up his sword arm and it glinted, menacingly, in the dull glow from the computer screens dotted around the space. The people in the room still did not lift their heads, not one of them.

'Move your arm out of the way, Doctor!' said Donna. 'Move it.'

The man grunted. 'This sword will go through them both, don't worry about that.'

'They're the worst kind of internet virus,' shouted the Doctor at the camera. 'You know it and I know it.'

Suddenly there was a buzz. A light above them in the ceiling, next to one of the cameras, gently flashed on, and then the camera started to whirr. The large man paused, his sword still held in the air.

There was a very long pause. The air was completely still apart from the humming of the room. And then: nothing.

The man holding Donna fast, appeared to make a decision and jerked up once more with the sword; its blade glinted above his huge head.

Donna and the Doctor shared only the briefest of glances, but it was enough. With a bang Donna kicked out to the side, and the Doctor tickled the man under his risen arm. The man twisted up and immediately collapsed down on the side, and the two of them dived away.

Unfortunately they dived in different directions.

Chapter
Fourteen

'Doctor!' shouted Donna, who stood at the door, ready to exit.

The Doctor by contrast was right on the other side of the room, banging on the other, steel door. They looked at each other in consternation.

'Oh, come on!' said Donna. 'Don't you think we should head out and regroup?'

'There's got to be someone in there,' the Doctor said, as the man recovered himself and stood up, a furious look on his face, spittle dripping from his lips. 'Good sword kicking by the way.'

'Thanks,' said Donna.

The man was clearly trying to advance on both of them, which was a difficult exercise, but he was looking from side to side, covering them with a gun he'd taken out of his pocket.

'So, what,' said the Doctor, staring at the pistol. 'You genuinely *preferred* to come at us with a sword?'

'Those are some serious issues you have,' said Donna, as the man's head whipped around. 'You should see a therapist of some kind. I mean, what do you even do with all those fingers?'

The man roared in anger and raised the gun to fire at the Doctor first. The Doctor ignored him, and knocked even harder on the door.

'Someone's in there,' he said. 'Someone knows what's going on.'

Donna was staring out at the rows of bent heads.

'Come *on*!' she implored them. 'One of you tell him to stop or get a policeman or something? Huh? Come on!'

Nothing moved. Nobody changed.

'Whatever happened to empathy?' shouted Donna.

The Doctor nodded at her. 'It's true. Normally in a crowd there'd be somebody. Somebody who'd help. It's normal human instinct. But here…'

The safety catch came off the gun.

'OK,' said Donna. 'Maybe we will go. Let's totally go. We're going! Bye! Doctor! *Come on!*'

'It is too late,' said the man. 'You have seen too many of the faces in this room. You can never leave.'

Donna tried the main door. It was locked.

The Doctor whirred round to gaze at the ceiling.

'Rempaths!' he roared suddenly. 'Rempaths are here! And if that doesn't frighten you, you've obviously never seen them in action.'

Once again the little camera blinked, once, twice, red, and whirred around to face the Doctor. Once again there was a silence in the room.

And then the man continued to advance, bearing down on them with the gun, covering first one, then another. Donna edged towards the Doctor, reaching out to grab his hand. The man bore down on them both, a huge mountainous figure over them, looming closer and closer as the sound of the people typing to drown them out stepped up a notch when…

There was a tiny click.

Chapter
Fifteen

The woman standing in front of the now-open door was rotund. Her face was covered in the pale white make-up Donna associated with geishas, but Donna couldn't imagine anyone less subservient-looking.

She was wearing a tightly wrapped *hanbok* in bright fuchsia pink on the bottom, and a paler pink on the shawl-like top, with a bright red ribbon hanging from it, and the bun in her hair, her open face and her squat rounded body reminded Donna, oddly, of a cake. The red ribbon she was wearing matched her sharply drawn lipstick. She smelled of something cucumbery, bright and herbal, sharp and unusual, and her face was strict, but kind, her cheeks round and highly rouged.

'Ian. Put the sword down, please. And the gun,' she said, quietly and rather nicely. 'Can't you see we have guests?'

She spoke in perfect English.

Donna glanced around. '*Ian?*' she said.

*

The heavy steel door clanged shut behind them, and they stepped into the most surprising room Donna could think of. Outside, the banks and rows of computer screens had been incredibly bland, and a surprise after the traditional decoration of the old building from the outside into a high-tech world within.

In here was quite the opposite. There must have been a side of the building, and the street, they had missed, for this room opened out into a huge space, all of it filled with greenery; bathed with light.

Palm trees and pot plants filled the space until it felt as if they were outside... and Donna saw, as she moved forwards, that there was an outside; that the room extended into an open courtyard with a vast garden beyond; there were raked gravel paths in the centre and plants all around. The pagoda-roofed buildings extended around a square. The greenery in the room they were in simply extended through the space out into the exterior. In one corner was a rock pool, in which fat orange fish darted lazily. A tiny, exquisitely fashioned wooden bridge arched over the babbling stream. Plucked music was playing, strange and low to Donna's ears.

Looking more carefully, Donna could see there were large screen doors that could be pulled in to separate the inside from the outside if it rained. Otherwise, it was an entirely harmonious marriage of the indoors and the outdoors, a soothing sound of running water coming from a little stream that fed the pond.

Down by their feet was a low lacquered table, set with mats and several lacquered teapots of varying sizes, from tiny through to an enormous specimen that appeared to be made of jade.

The woman blinked at them. She didn't speak, merely indicated the set table with her head.

'Who are you? What's going on? Who's Ian?' said Donna immediately, her heart still racing from their narrow escape.

But both the Doctor and the woman hushed her with a look.

Very calmly and in total silence, they sat down cross-legged and took their places at the low table. The Doctor genuflected his head a little as the woman unhurriedly began to heat up the water for tea. It boiled over sweetly scented cedar wood that burned on a little brazier.

Donna was almost bouncing with frustration. But time passed and still nobody spoke, and so, instead of sitting down like the Doctor, she went out into the garden to walk around.

In the garden everything was ordered.

The noise from the street was muffled here amongst the patches of wild grasses that were sown at careful intervals, and retreated into gentle white noise. The babble of the stream was calming; so were the paths that led through the garden in gentle twisting knots. Every corner of the path seemed to lead to another perfectly framed vista against the red pagodas or carefully raked stones; squares of gently weaving lavender scenting the air, or straight-planted rows of bonsai trees. The only thing she noticed that stood out was something shaped like a manhole cover, that seemed to be exuding a faint blue light. Or perhaps it was simply the way the sun dappled through the leaves.

Donna glanced back into the room behind her. Framed by the outline of the screen doors, the Doctor and the lady were now involved in a small intense ritual of moving cups; sieving green tea through ornate strainers, and, finally, pouring it from a great height, where it gently bubbled down into the exquisite china.

As she watched she felt an unfamiliar feeling steal over her; calm. Her heart rate slowed. Her shoulders untangled themselves from up somewhere around her ears.

The Doctor and the woman were performing an act that had not changed for thousands of years. It gave Donna hope, somewhere, somehow, that it would not change for thousands more.

Calmer now, Donna re-entered the light-filled room, and even though still not a word had yet been spoken, she felt welcomed back at a new, slower pace. She then tried to sit down on the cushions provided in front of the low table; something the Doctor had managed with no little grace, but to her felt like she was getting into trouble in primary school and being made to sit cross-legged at the front of assembly.

Finally a handmade cup of steaming, fragrant tea was set in front of her. There was a bud in it. As she watched, the flower unfolded itself in the hot water, and the soft scent of jasmine spread in the room. She watched what the others did and then carefully, respectfully, with both hands she lifted the earthenware cup and took a small sip. The taste was delicate, unusual and highly refreshing in the sunlit room. Suddenly Donna felt that she wanted to lie down and sleep for a hundred years. She had never felt so far away from the frenetic modern world.

'Thank you,' said the Doctor, bowing his head deeply, and Donna nodded in agreement.

'Ji Woo,' said the woman.

'Donna Noble,' said Donna.

The woman bowed her head. 'And...' she said. Her eyes were dark and penetrating and she turned her head to stare straight at the Doctor. 'I have a theory,' she said, 'as to who you are. Are you aware of a Clive Finch from England?'

The Doctor shook his head.

'He had a website.'

The Doctor looked at her.

'Do you control all the websites in the world?' asked Donna.

The woman shook her head, smiling. 'Oh no. Some pique my interest more than others.'

'But you deal in websites...?' Donna realised she had only the haziest idea how the internet actually worked.

'I deal in exchanges,' said the woman, sipping her tea. 'Between the old world and the new. I cannot help the new world coming, Doctor. Nobody can. I am here and I facilitate.'

The Doctor blinked. 'You form it, every single person on Earth. You forge your own future.'

The woman shook her head. 'Oh, I am merely caught up in the slipstream.'

The Doctor gave her a shrewd look. 'I think we both know that's not true.'

Donna glanced at the locked steel door. 'Why are all those people lined up back there, like they're doing school detention? Who are they?'

'This is the safest, the most private, the fastest internet space on Earth,' said Ji Woo. 'Here we have a completely clean space. It is utterly unhackable by anybody outside it. We have our own cable, our own network, our own completely sealed-off private online universe. Nobody can get in and nobody can get out. Only very specially selected clients may apply. The cost is… astronomical. But there is no remote access. To anything. Everyone must be in the same space at the same time, so nobody who is involved could ever possibly infiltrate anybody else without us instantly being aware. No hacking. No undercutting. Physical presence only.'

'Who are they?' said the Doctor.

Ji Woo shook her head and carefully poured more tea. 'Why on earth would we ask?'

'And you don't care what they talk about, what they're doing in there?'

'I'm just providing a service, albeit highly specialised,' said Ji Woo. 'Like every other internet provider in the world. I'm not responsible for what they do.'

Donna frowned. 'I don't buy that.'

'Do you use an internet provider?'

'Yeah, but…'

'Well then I can tell you beyond a shadow of a doubt that you do indeed "buy that".' Ji Woo slightly tittered, and hid her mouth with a napkin. 'You probably give your date of birth away for free Wi-Fi.'

'She does,' said the Doctor. 'I'm always telling her.'

Donna pouted.

The Doctor turned back to Ji Woo. 'You know something has come. Something is here; something is inside your "clean" pathways. You have a hitchhiker. You know what the Rempaths are?'

Ji Woo shrugged carefully and did not reply.

The Doctor set down his cup. 'They are travelling along your roads, Ji Woo. Your cold, brutal pathways. Your silk roads, your shadow paths: each of them paved with the crushed skulls of the innocents who got lost along the way.'

'So you would kill the road builders, Doctor? Perhaps the architects too, just to be safe?'

'If I can't stop this, Manim, I won't have to. The Rempaths will do that for me.'

'Stop it?' laughed Ji Woo. 'You can't *stop it*, any more than you can stop the wind. So many people out there, Doctor. Wanting so many things. Wanting, wanting, wanting. Terrible things they want. Terrible things. And they get so cross. So angry, so frustrated when they don't get what they want. So I give them what they want; that is all.'

'Have you tried raising a child that way?' said the Doctor, bitterly. 'You won't like what you get.'

'Have you?' returned Ji Woo, without looking up from her cup.

There was a long silence.

'You run this business,' said the Doctor, finally. 'But you don't own it. I reckon you couldn't pull the plug here even if you wanted to.'

'Why would I want to?' said Ji Woo. 'History comes and history goes, but some of us remain. I am Korean, Doctor. Very little scares me.'

'Tell me who runs this place.'

Ji Woo smiled. 'Ah, Doctor. I don't employ Ian for nothing.'

'You don't employ him at all,' said the Doctor. 'Someone else pulls the strings of all of this, don't they? Otherwise you'd probably have employed someone with more of a brain in his head.'

'Yeah, you should tell him to watch out for sword kicking,' said Donna. 'Seriously, that's like, day two of sword school.'

Ji Woo blinked. 'There are many, many Ians,' she said. 'Consider him our entry-level expendable. Although Clive Finch suggested that isn't how you operate.' She held his gaze. 'And yet you are still considered highly dangerous. Isn't that strange?'

'Isn't it?' said the Doctor.

Donna looked suddenly into the corner of the room. Behind a vast and green bank of ferns, several CCTV cameras were monitoring the main room and the street beyond – where, she now noticed, people she had thought were restaurateurs scanning the street for custom were clearly lookouts. They had been expected all along.

She looked back into the room. The rows of people were still typing, intently, each buried in the private universe their screens afforded them, each its own world to them where they carried out their business, whether drug running or slave trading or terrorism... who could say? Who knew? Someone started and glanced behind them; as if they had felt a draft.

Her eye was caught by a younger girl, beautiful, who looked South American. She was dressed immaculately, very high-end white designer gear, in which she fitted perfectly; with a bag with a huge branded logo; shoes that cost more than Donna had spent on her wedding dress, which was just as well, she thought, in retrospect.

She looked more closely. The woman was frowning at her computer screen. Her elegantly shod leg in its tight white jeans was kicking out, a repeated nervous tic.

The Doctor and Ji Woo were still pouring tea, sitting in a perfect facsimile of politeness. Donna moved closer to the screen. The woman was typing now furiously, her face a mask of anger.

'Doctor,' said Donna, in a warning voice.

He glanced up. Ji Woo's head turned.

Now the woman was gesticulating, shouting at the screen. Her leg accidentally kicked someone else on the opposite side of the desk. Now that man had stood up, and was shouting back at her. She stood up too.

The warm sunlit room chilled suddenly; as if a cloud had appeared. Even the cooing birds seemed to go quiet.

It happened so fast.

There was no noise on the CCTV. But you didn't need noise to know that the delicate diplomatic balance that held sway amongst that room of the misbegotten had gone.

Now you could see people's faces, filled with rage and fury. Spittle flew in the air. Two men in the far corner squared up to one another. It was becoming obvious that blows were about to be struck. Ian turned his head towards the camera in consternation. He obviously had orders not to discipline his paying customers. Ji Woo looked at it intently.

A very small, young-looking chap who Donna had hardly noticed on the end of the row darted up, frightened suddenly. He charged towards the door. Before he got there, someone had tripped him up.

'Oh my…' said Donna.

'Open the door,' ordered the Doctor, now standing, trying to pull open the steel. 'Open it now. We can still save some of them.'

On the CCTV in the corner one man grabbed at his chest. His mouth opened in a soundless howl and he clutched himself, froze, and then began to fall. The rest of the people in the room completely ignored him, continuing to fight one another. Someone bit someone else. Ian was pounding on the door now.

The Doctor grabbed his sonic and worked on the locked door, but Ji Woo simply leaned over – her face now had lost all its grandmotherly friendliness and was a pale white-painted mask – and pressed her fingertip on a control panel. Instantly, great big sheets of steel began to descend at high speed from the ceiling, covering the walls.

'No!' shouted Donna. The pounding on the other side of the door grew louder.

'Let me in! Let me in!' came Ian's voice, desperate now. There was an increasing hubbub.

The Doctor frowned, desperately working on the door. But the metal sheets were falling faster and faster every second. The beautiful sunlight and the garden were vanishing like a dream. The room darkened.

'Doctor!' yelled Donna, and at last he gave up his fruitless efforts on opening the door, his face in agony.

Instead he turned in consternation towards the back part of the room, the side that led out to the garden. The steel had nearly hit the ground. He glanced around the room quickly, weighing and measuring at lightning speed in his mind. Finally he grabbed the largest, beautifully glazed jade teapot; the precious antique, patinated by generations of traditions over the years; a sacred household object, handed down through families.

He grabbed it and hurled it beneath the crushing metal where the doors opened on to the garden. There was a juddering, tearing noise, and the wall continued to descend, the teapot giving, and softening. Until, as the room watched, it buckled a little… and then there was a judder and a sound of crunching gears and, not half a metre from the bottom, the door froze. The rest of what was clearly a panic room was now sheeted in metal.

Ji Woo strode towards them both. 'I'm afraid you may not leave now,' she said.

Donna could no longer watch the horrifying CCTV footage. She couldn't bear it any longer and leaned over and covered the screens with her jacket.

Ji Woo carefully bent down to pull out the teapot from the still grinding metal wall.

'Oh no you don't!' shouted Donna, and grabbed another pot. She lifted it up high.

'This is boiling!' she said, dashing to her and holding it up. 'You move and it's going right over your face and… melting it. Ugh.'

Ji Woo made a small smile. 'Getting angry, are we? I hear that is not terribly useful.'

'No,' Donna said. 'I'm completely calm about what I have to do to immobilise you.'

The Doctor had already dashed over and pressed the fingerprint screen to raise the doors. Nothing happened.

Ji Woo looked at him. 'You're not me,' she said, the hint of a smile playing on her lips.

'Thank goodness,' said the Doctor, roughly. 'Come here and press it, please.'

'And condemn myself to death?'

The Doctor blinked. All three of them in the room suddenly were silent, looking at one another.

'Oh, Ji Woo,' said the Doctor. 'I'm so sorry. But you know. Whatever happens. You are already condemned to death.'

There was a pause.

The Doctor shook his head. 'You knew all along. You facilitated this.' He looked her straight in the face. 'You have more than one paymaster, don't you? Those... wretches...' He indicated the door beyond. 'Well. They've gone. But there's someone else, isn't there?'

He indicated the screens, then crouched and looked at the manhole shaped disc in the garden, which was now pulsing its blue light.

'Perhaps they're a little... unusual, maybe? Or maybe you haven't met them? Just through an intermediary?'

Ji Woo's face sagged suddenly, and she seemed older, but tried to look resolute, even with Donna holding up the kettle. 'He will know my discretion was absolute.'

'Oh, he won't care,' said the Doctor.

'I shan't let him down.'

'Too late,' said the Doctor. 'It's simply too late.'

There was a buzzing from the other room of computers starting up. As they did so, the manhole began to pulse even more strongly with the blue light.

'You didn't need me to tell you what Rempaths are,' he said, coldly. 'You knew that all right. You just didn't know whose side *I* was on.'

Ji Woo's expression didn't change.

'Oh, Ji Woo,' said the Doctor. 'Never yours.'

The Doctor looked at the jade teapot creaking under the metal wall and back at the round figure of Ji Woo. 'You can't fit under that gap.'

'I'm sure you'd say I don't deserve to.'

Already, the CCTV cameras were showing a mass of men in uniforms – not police, and not national soldiers either, but something more akin to a private army – amassing on the road outside the shop. Their faces were grave.

'Go,' said the Doctor to Donna. She squeezed herself under with some difficulty, but was relieved when he didn't offer to give her a shove. In fact, when she glanced back underneath, she saw him looking back at Ji Woo.

'I walk a lonely road,' she was muttering to herself.

The Doctor nodded as if he understood, and perhaps he did.

Ji Woo moved herself back to the low table. The beautiful tea pot they had used was still there. Ji Woo sat back down again, blinking rapidly, and, with a trembling hand, poured herself a last cup of tea.

'삶이 있는 동안 희망은 있다. 살아있는 한 희망은 있다,' said the Doctor, but Ji Woo looked around only once, and merely shook her head.

The Doctor glanced for the last time at the darkened room, the seated woman, the horrifying tableau – still, now – of what was left of the inhabitants of the computer room, seemingly frozen on the CCTV screen. Then he heard the rapping and barked 'Open up' commands of the militia men.

'Doctor, hurry up!' shouted Donna. 'They're coming! Come on!'

The moment hung on the air; quivered. Outside, banging was heard and shots were fired into the air. Ji Woo tilted her head and stared straight at the Doctor. When she spoke, it was almost a whisper.

'The Ice King,' she said. 'The land of the Ice King.'

There was a huge bursting noise as the door to the building was flung open and, on the CCTV, men poured into the first room, gasping at the stacked corpses they found there. The noise grew louder. A banging started at the inner door.

The Doctor nodded once more, and sprinted lightly to the space, rolled under and into the bright daylight. He grabbed Donna's hand, and they tore across the garden, up the narrow crenelated wall and away, as the brightly coloured birds rose from the trees, startled from their peaceful afternoon, and lifted, circling and cawing into the sky. Below, the armed men, overseen by a man in sunglasses, brought out their metal cutters and started to attack the steel door, sparks flying in the room of horrors, and Ji Woo, for the final time, carefully put down her beautifully lacquered earthenware cup.

Chapter
Sixteen

'Seriously,' said the Doctor. 'This is awful. This isn't a rogue virus. This is an industry. Someone brought it; released it into the system, like dropping cholera into the water supply.'

He sighed.

'And Ji Woo was harvesting it. She leased her secure lines to whoever wanted them, and they were the perfect conduit to spread the thing out across the world.' He winced. 'So, presumably if nobody liked looking up really awful things on the internet, none of this would have happened.'

They'd found a small restaurant back on the Gangnam side of the river, in a bustling business district full of international travellers, where nobody was giving them a second glance. The Doctor was studying a map he'd bought in a bookstore.

'Ice King,' mused Donna. 'That's really inconvenient. It could mean the very top end or the very bottom. Like, totally a world apart. I don't suppose she mentioned whether he had penguins or polar bears with him?'

The Doctor shook his head. 'I don't think she actually meant that he's somewhere icy. I think that's just what he does to his victims. The feeling of ice inside your heart.'

Donna blinked. 'So, where are we going, then?'

The Doctor started folding the flat world map, rapidly and carefully making creases on separate angles.

Donna watched him, bemused. 'What are you doing? I thought origami was Japanese.'

But he didn't listen and when he looked up he had turned the flat map into a perfect three dimensional globe. It was beautiful.

'Ooh, show-off,' said Donna. 'Can I have it for a lampshade?'

The Doctor didn't answer but instead spun it around and pointed to a spot on the map. 'I think he might be there.'

'Why would he be there?'

'I don't know. A weird theory I have.'

'This is quite a lot of air tickets to buy on a theory.'

'You have to *pay* to go on one of those things?'

Donna blinked. 'You know, it's weird when you think about it, but yes. Loads!' She let her finger trace the map. 'Look, we'll probably have to change at Heathrow anyway.'

'Your travelling arrangements are so peculiar. Why do you have to keep stopping to buy all those triangles? Why do they make you do that?'

'What triangles?'

'When they make you get off a plane to pay money for triangles. It's just so peculiar.'

Donna thought about it for a bit. 'Do you mean Toblerone?' she said eventually.

The Doctor nodded.

'Oh,' said Donna. 'I've never really thought about it.'

'I can tell.'

'Well,' said Donna, folding her arms. 'It's the only way to get there. And we have to have a layover at Heathrow. So I'm going to see Gramps.'

The news showed them nothing cheerier. Everything was speeding up the faster the Rempaths were moving. And the papers were full of stories; people were dying, young, after going online. They were calling it Webmageddon. The Trollpocalypse.

You would think, the Doctor pondered, leafing through the press, that this would stop people going online. But it didn't seem to be having any effect at all. On the contrary: vast flame wars had broken out all over the internet assigning blame for the deaths to a variety of causes, including vaccination, GM food and an assortment of political parties. One or two of the more tinfoil hat websites were even close to getting it right.

He frowned, and glanced over at Donna, who was busying herself with her phone. 'Oi! Are you online?'

'I'm reposting some motivational messages,' said Donna stoutly, sharing a picture of a kitten looking over the sea at the sunset. 'To cheer people up and stop them getting so angry on the internet.'

'I'm not sure those things don't make people quite annoyed,' said the Doctor.

'Well some people are never happy,' said Donna, liking every single photograph she came across in an effort to increase the sum of online politeness.

'No,' said the Doctor, musing. 'Come on. You're throwing water in a bucket with a hole in it. Let's get going.'

Chapter
Seventeen

The Australian drummed his fingers crossly on the desk. They were on the webcam.

'Nothing?' he said.

'Nothing,' said the man with the yellow eyes, sitting high up in the bright shiny office in Seoul, the sun blazing in, the stark interior lines hard and clean. His militia men had long gone.

The old man on the other end of the line, skin rough as a lizard's, blinked, slowly. 'But you caught her?'

'She gave nothing up.'

'Even to you?'

This was what the man was paid for. He was relentless in his questioning; repetitive and never deviating or letting up for an instant. It generally never failed. People flailed, got upset, became emotional. It was normally very quick.

Not her. He had done things to her... well. It was fortunate this particular office had plastic sheeting. And blackout blinds. And soundproofing, although he hadn't needed that. She hadn't made a sound the entire time. He had never come across anything quite like it. There was, it seemed, absolutely nothing he could do to her. There was no way she was going to talk. No way at all.

There was no record of any family, any connections. There was absolutely no record of her existence at all. He didn't even know her name.

But she had been there, after the fool and his sidekick had led him right to what he was looking for. They'd shown him the way. The people who'd died there; he'd found all of them on a watch list easily enough. Major terrorists; people smugglers; gun runners. The scum of humanity, all of them, and all of them known at the high levels of penetration of his own organisation.

But this woman... nothing. And absolutely nothing he could do to her seemed to be changing anything about that. It was as if she had slipped into a trance; her pulse rate was barely noticeable. As if anything he did to the body was completely separate to wherever she was inside her mind.

'I think she must have been playing both sides,' he said, quietly.

The Australian chuckled; a dry, barking noise. 'What, there's someone she's more scared of than us? Sheesh, I wouldn't like to meet him,' he said. 'What happened to the other two?'

'They ducked out. I have men on all the airport and ferry feeds. But if I couldn't get anything out of her...'

'Don't take anything for granted,' warned the Australian.

'I never do,' said the man.

'Get it sorted.'

'I will.'

Chapter
Eighteen

Chiswick felt dull and grey after the bright sharp sunlight of Seoul. Donna had left the Doctor on triangle-testing duty and had slipped into a cab.

'Oh, there you are,' said Sylvia, coming out to the doorstep. 'Treating this house like a hotel, as usual. Are you working or travelling or what? Your fringe is getting too long.'

'It's nice to see you too, Mum.'

'Seriously, do you want me to cut it?'

Donna blinked. 'You really have missed me.'

Donna sat in the familiar small kitchen with its orange curtains whilst her mother came at her with the kitchen scissors.

'Where's Gramps?'

'In the shed,' said her mother, in a resigned tone. 'Keeps him out from under my feet. Anyway, he's extended the wiffy connection out there.'

'The what?'

'You know. Wiffy.'

'Do you mean Wi-Fi?'

'Yes. You know. The weird stuff that floats in the air.'

'And he's got it in his *shed*?'

'I know, it's not right.'

Donna jumped up.

'Hang on, I'm not finished!'

'That's OK, it'll give you something to complain about next time. And give me those scissors.'

Donna knocked gently on the door of the shed. Wilf opened the door tentatively, then his kindly white-bearded face broke into the widest of smiles as he saw his favourite granddaughter. He flung his arms around her.

'Donna! It's so… it is. Well. It is quite lovely to see you. What's up with your hair?'

'Don't worry about that right now. What are you doing back here?'

Donna looked at his old computer on the desk, now blinking cheerfully with the familiar little fan of lines indicating that it was connected. 'Gramps. You have to disconnect from the internet.' She held up the scissors. 'Show me the box. I know they say wireless, but there's always one around somewhere.'

Wilf sighed. 'This is your mum again, isn't it? Tell her again: I'm not looking at mucky pictures.'

Donna shook her head. 'It's not that, Gramps. It's… well, have you heard of a computer virus?'

Wilf shrugged. 'The salesman said something…'

'Well,' said Donna. 'It's a bit like that. But not that. But it's still important. You have to come offline. Now. Sorry. You can totally still play patience.'

Wilf looked downhearted. 'But this is... this is where I log in my stars. You know. I like to see what's up there, and anything unusual I log it with SETI and then I can chat to people there who are looking at the sky like me... It's nice. I don't feel lonely, even with you away.' He glanced at her slyly. 'Of course I never let on *who* I'm looking for.'

Donna smiled.

Wilf looked at his computer sadly and cleared his throat. 'How's that tall friend of yours?'

'Same as ever. Off his head. But in the best possible way.'

Wilf gave her a shrewd look. 'You're not going sweet on him, are you? Because I know what you're like with the boys.'

'Gramps!'

'I remember you in primary school. Any game of kiss-chase, you'd either started it or were willingly losing right in the middle of it...'

Donna rolled her eyes.

'I'm only thinking of you sweetheart. You know that.'

'I know, Gramps. And no, honestly. I promise. I couldn't. I really couldn't. It would be like falling in love with a walrus or a tiger or something. I really, properly couldn't. Actually. There was someone. A person, I mean. A real person. Well, he wasn't...

I mean, real is. Well. Never mind. But it didn't work out.'

Wilf patted her hand. 'You know, ducks, when I met your grandmother, I just knew. Within seconds. It felt like we'd been together for ever. And the time we had together, it flew. It just flew past, like a year would take a minute. You know, when you have that, you just know. It went far too fast.'

Donna nodded slowly. 'OK.'

Wilf looked at her. 'Is it really important, this internet thing?'

Donna nodded. 'Yes. It really is. If you saw anything that made you angry...'

'I'm too old to get angry,' said Wilf. 'I did my anger in the war. Nothing I can do these days. Just watch and nod. I've seen it all before.'

'I know,' said Donna. 'I know that. But just in case.'

She gave him a hug. He sighed.

'What?' said Donna.

'I know that hug,' said Wilf. 'It means you're off again, doesn't it? It's your "off again" hug. It means you're going to be leaving me out here in my shed, all by myself, without even my online mates to talk to.'

'I'm sorry,' said Donna, and she was. Because she loved him and she knew he loved her. But she was still going to go.

'Don't you want me to finish your fringe?' shouted Sylvia as she was leaving. 'Honestly, you're so ungrateful for everything.'

'I know,' said Donna. 'Sorry. In a rush. Got a plane to catch.'

Sylvia came to the door, clutching a box of Tupperware. She looked nervous. 'Um...' she said. 'I put together some leftovers. In this box. I knew... I knew you probably wouldn't be staying for supper.'

Donna looked up at her. 'Thanks,' she said.

There was a pause.

'So give me some notice next time,' said Sylvia. 'Some of us are busy, you know.'

Donna gave a half-smile. 'I know,' she said, and took the box with thanks, then turned round and wandered out into the rain.

She took a detour on her way to the Piccadilly line back to Heathrow, down the row of the big grand houses by the river. Nobody was about, except the usual rich people's street population: cleaners; foreign nannies wearily pushing buggies that cost more than they earned in a month; gardeners and delivery van drivers, none of whom gave her a second glance.

She stopped outside Hettie's house, with its spotless white steps and perfectly manicured little trees lining the tiny balconies. She glanced around. Nobody.

Nonchalantly, she moved over to the telegraph pole and took out the sonic she'd asked properly to borrow this time. The Doctor had been very not at all keen and had made her promise several times not to put it in her handbag – seeing as things scattered about all the time – and wanted her to call in every half an hour and confirm she still had it and went to great and tortuously dull lengths to remind her not to touch the blue settings or disengage the new dampers.

By the time he'd finished pacing about and agonising, she was totally wishing she'd not asked to borrow it and just brought a hammer instead. It would have done the same job without anything like the grief.

Regardless, she lifted it up towards the telecoms box on the pole, and flashed it once, twice. Instantly there was a buzz and a crackle. Then, silence. Then, a few moments later, muffled cursing and lights being turned on and off in different rooms.

Donna resealed the control box, so technicians would have an impossible job trying to get into it, then stole away.

Chapter
Nineteen

'Thank you for your patience,' the young man was saying earnestly over the web. The older man blinked, not removing his glasses.

The young man was nervous, of course. Everyone in the Australian organisation was always nervous. The entire business ran on jangling nerves and fear and favour and seniority.

But this time, unusually, it was the man with the yellow eyes who had failed; who had not been able to break the old woman, who had looked so sweet; like a little round doll.

She hadn't made a sound, not even with her dying breath.

Appearances could be deceiving. Not his appearance, though. He knew that, and quickly tapped his glasses.

Hence the quivering boy, whose fear could be felt even over the internet connection; the fact that they were thousands of miles apart didn't seem to lessen the effect of his presence in the slightest. He adjusted his earpiece.

'And?'

'We… we think we've seen them.'

Another screen opened up showing CCTV footage of Donna and the Doctor heading through Heathrow Airport. The camera zoomed in on their faces, and subtitles came up underneath them.

'He talks a lot,' observed the man.

'They both do, sir,' said the intern. 'It's giving the lip readers all sorts of headaches.'

Regardless, this was clearly the opportune moment.

'The *other* great thing about Rio,' the man was saying, gesticulating with his arms as the woman with the oddly cut hair put her bag through the X-ray machine. The man didn't seem to have any baggage at all.

'The *other* great thing about Rio is—'

'I mean it, if you don't stop banging on about Rio, I'm going to change planes for Scarborough,' said the woman. And the intern froze the screen.

'I think that's us, sir.'

'Unless they're bluffing,' said the man.

The intern zoomed in again on the two boarding passes hanging out of Donna's pocket. 'Expensive bluff, sir.'

The man folded his arms. 'Fine. Get me booked there asap. Different flights, they're a menace to public transportation.'

Chapter
Twenty

The ancient train – once a workhorse of South America, now adapted into a luxurious steam trip for tourists – puffed its way happily under the setting sun in the clear skies over the dramatic Serra da Mantiqueira.

The Doctor lounged comfortably in his seat. It was the oddest thing, given that he had not enjoyed air travel in the slightest. But here, on the great Brazilian Scenic railway, travelling about a twentieth as fast, he looked entirely at ease.

It might be, Donna thought, the soft deep leather armchairs they were travelling in; the dark wooden panelling on the walls; the beautiful, deep burgundy cars. It was like travelling back in time without actually having to go to the trouble of doing it. And with flushing toilets.

The train had left Rio de Janeiro that morning and was now trundling over a narrow mountainous passageway, where they went so close to the edge she felt in danger of the entire structure tumbling off into the fluffy clouds below. They had booked too late for two separate cabins, and were limited to bunk beds in the same space.

Donna hadn't yet decided which was best, top or bottom bunk, and was feeling rather nervous about it. The Doctor had been delighted, which meant she should probably let him have the top. Where they were headed was deep into the jungle, and this was the best way through.

They were sitting in the grand dining car, with its regency striped wallpaper and hardwood tables, and a waiter in tails had taken their cocktail orders. Donna had glanced around, hoping vaguely that perhaps James Bond would be sitting at a table in the corner, possibly thinking how he hadn't met a red-headed Bond girl for absolutely ages, and he would be drinking his cocktail, feeling lonely and wishing someone would actually walk into the dangerously swaying carriage, and then she'd walk down the aisle, and possibly be pushed up against him with one sudden motion of the carriage as it turned a corner, and he'd throw out his arm to steady her and…

'What are you thinking about?' said the Doctor.

'Um… I'm thinking about how to solve this. Obviously.' said Donna, quickly. She took a sip of her martini. It was perfect. 'I mean, why can't they just shut down the internet? Just stop it happening?'

The Doctor shrugged. 'If it's civil disorder and violence you're trying to avoid, shutting down the internet is absolutely the last thing you should do. They'd be fighting in the streets in ten seconds flat.'

'Do you really think so?'

'Absolutely. I think repressed violence is probably better than actual violence for now.'

'Really? But if we know it's going to kill people...'

'Why do you think they still let people eat sugar? We know it kills them.'

'Yes, but this is killing people *right now*.'

'Donna, there's a smoking carriage on this train.'

Donna fell silent and took another sip of her martini. 'Well, there you go. You asked what I was thinking and there it is. I told Gramps about it. I hope he listens.'

The Doctor smiled.

'What?'

'Donna, if anyone's immune, it's Wilf.'

Donna blinked. 'Do you think?'

'There isn't an ounce of aggression in him, as far as I can tell.'

'But people can be immune?' said Donna, interested now, sitting up.

'Oh well, maybe not immune exactly, but not everyone will get it, yeah. Just by dialling with your anger online, working on your better self, trying to eliminate your faults and listening to your conscience... You know, good manners?'

Donna blinked. 'Wow, you sound like an old book.'

'I know,' said the Doctor, pushing up his glasses and staring out of the window. 'I'm wildly out of fashion. They renamed basic species empathy as "political correctness gone mad", and the world's never been the same since. Dunno why.'

Donna nodded. 'Yeah, everyone's got to "say things straight" to you these days.' She thought about it. 'I dunno why either.' She looked over at him. His head was leaning on the window, still gazing out at the extraordinary passing scenery. 'Are you immune?'

The Doctor took a sip of his Old Fashioned. He didn't say anything for a while.

'Why do you think I need the two hearts?' he said finally.

Chapter
Twenty-One

The train thundered on into the night, through the dark valleys of Southern Brazil, the mountain peaks great points in the night, blocking out triangles of stars. There were blackout blinds on the cabin window, but by unspoken agreement they'd left them open to look out on the night as the great engine rattled along, the carriage gently swaying.

It was still very dark in the small panelled room. Donna realised she didn't think she had the faintest possibility of managing to get to sleep in this. It felt suddenly very peculiar trying to sleep with someone else – a lanky big alien, no less – in the same room. She turned over in the dark, pondering.

'Do you sleep?' she shouted up eventually.

'Through all this shouting? Wouldn't have thought so,' returned the voice. 'Want some Toblerone?'

'I've brushed my teeth already! Haven't you?'

There was no answer. But there was a quiet tinny rustle of Toblerone being unwrapped.

Donna sighed. 'Chuck us a bit, then.'

'I thought you'd brushed your teeth.'

'Teeth can be rebrushed.'

'Not those teeth. Don't you dare.'

Donna thought she could feel him smile in the darkness, and smiled quietly to herself in response. If she could heal after Lee…

Well. At least the Doctor would never meet that troublesome woman again. She couldn't bear him sad. They would both recover from The Library, she knew, in time. There was a whole universe out there, of fun, of excitement. All they had to do first was fix the entire world's internet, and then they'd be off again and fine, and everything would be fun and normal again, i.e. terrifying and completely abnormal.

She lay back and closed her eyes. Then she opened them again.

'What is it now?' said the Doctor, as if he'd heard her eyelids open. Which he probably had.

'It's no use,' said Donna. 'My teeth are all sticky. I'm not going to be able to fall asleep. I remember at school, right, they dropped a tooth into a cup of fizzy drink, and Mrs Higgins said, now children this is what will happen to you if you don't….'

She paused. Slow steady breathing came from the top bunk.

'Are you pretending to be asleep?' she said crossly.

There was the very mildest of tiny snores.

When the banging came, Donna shot up in bed, completely disorientated, adrenalin pulsing through her veins. She was in her pyjamas not knowing what bed, what country, what planet she was on. All she knew was that the room was shaking, and that she thought she'd heard a great noise – or had it been a dream?

Lightly, the figure of the Doctor landed next to her.

The banging was at the door. It did not sound friendly.

'I'll press for the attendant,' she said, stupidly, her voice sounding heavy as she attempted to shake herself awake.

'Come in?' the Doctor was saying. 'Although I don't recall ordering room service… You, Donna?'

'No,' said Donna, awake finally. 'Although I wish I had… Do you think they'll make us a coffee?'

The door banged open. Standing there was the huge man they'd last seen in a tiny smelly room in West London, picking up computers as if they were feathers. He blocked the light from the corridor. Donna quickly glanced in case there was anything in the tiny cabin she could use as a weapon. There was some leftover tin foil, but that was about it.

He was still wearing dark glasses, even though it was the dead of night as far as Donna could tell.

'Someone's going to hear you,' blurted out Donna. As she spoke the train gave a huge hoot as it went into a long tunnel. The window became completely black and the noise levels extraordinary. Nobody could hear anything.

'I thought you said you were the police,' said the Doctor. 'What is this, Interpol?'

The man stared at them for a moment. 'Yeah, that's right, I'm the police.'

'You're not the police!' said Donna.

'Oh yeah, because you are?' the man grunted. He came in and sat down on the lower bunk.

'Get out of my bed!' shouted Donna.

The man shot her a glance. 'Or what? You're going to report me to Internal Affairs?' The direction of his gaze changed, as if he were no longer interested in her. 'So,' he said. 'This is all very helpful, well done, etcetera.'

He was addressing the Doctor, who had folded his arms impatiently.

'And far enough now, don't you think?'

The Doctor blinked.

'I appreciate an enthusiastic amateur as much as anyone, but I think it's time you let the professionals take over... and tell me why you're on the trail.'

'*Amateurs?*' said the Doctor.

'It's true, we don't take cash,' said Donna.

'You're appalling at going undercover,' said the man.

'Actually, normally I'm brilliant at it,' said the Doctor. 'I'm quite the master of facial disguise. And my ship is pretty impenetrable too. But *somebody* gave my ship away to some *baristas*—'

'It was very good coffee,' said Donna.

'—So now I'm... yes. Not exactly travelling incognito.'

The train was still rocketing through the tunnel, the wind shrieking past the window at a tremendous pace.

'But I think you're getting close, don't you?'

The Doctor stared straight ahead.

'She told you, didn't she?' said the man.

'I don't know what you're talking about.'

'She told you. Where to find whoever's behind this. Because there's something very badly up with the computers. And the people who spend a lot of time on them. But it's not some spotty hacker in a back room in Seoul or Dakar or Palo Alto, is it?'

The Doctor shook his head. 'No.'

The man nodded. 'Where is it?'

'Who are you?'

'Oh please, let's just get on. I've wasted enough time. A lot of time. Do you know how many of my people are dead?'

'Your people?' said the Doctor.

'Other policemen?' said Donna.

'Donna, he's not a policeman!' said the Doctor.

The man ignored her. 'Yes,' he said. 'Our people. Our customers. There are… many vested interests at work here. All that repressed anger… that rage; that fury at modern society…' He paused, breathing slowly and steadily, the same relaxed set to his features. 'It belongs to us. And we want it back.'

And he did a very surprising thing. He handed over his business card.

Chapter
Twenty-Two

The Doctor looked at the man's card, astounded.

'You're in the *media* business?'

'It's quite cutthroat.'

'And what are you doing?'

'The media is dying, Doctor. Dying all around us. The traditional ways of getting the news – they're gone. The internet is eating all of it. And regurgitating it up in little bullet points and fake memes and fake news reports and conspiracy theories and a constant swirling mass of rumour and fuss and fear. So our job now – those left with jobs – is to provide consumers with everything they need to get upset about.'

The Doctor blinked and held up his hands in a gesture of despair. 'What? Who cares! People are getting killed!'

'Yes,' said the man. 'Our readers.' He leaned forward. 'And it's multibillion-dollar business. You know what happens to us if people stop getting angry and upset at the things on the internet? If they stop commenting on newspaper articles in case they die? We die. My media outlet dies.'

'This is the stupidest thing I've ever heard,' said Donna.

'Have you never clicked on a link that suggests your country machine-guns migrants? Or takes children away from fat parents? Or that women should stay at home and look after their children?'

'Yeah, but…'

'Have you ever got upset about them?'

'Of course.'

'Have you ever commented on them?'

Donna shrugged. 'Isn't it… isn't it kind of for losers?'

'Losers give us clicks, which gives us money… They comment and click all the time, and build views up and advertising rates up, and that's how it all works.'

'So your business plan is based on upsetting already unhappy people?' said Donna, aghast.

'Yes,' said the man. 'Like, you know, Zumba.'

'And you're telling me your employer would actually hurt people to stop this?' said the Doctor.

'Have you met many media barons?' said the man.

'Fair point.'

'So,' said the man. 'We want the same thing. To stop this. It seems to make more sense now if we join up? Before I thought you were just useless. But now I figure you're getting somewhere.'

'Where's Ji Woo?'

'Who?'

The Doctor and Donna exchanged glances.

'She didn't even tell you her name?' said Donna.

'That woman in Korea?' said the man, his face twisting. 'She was the real criminal. Ji Woo sanctioned things you wouldn't believe.'

The Doctor blinked. 'Where is she?'

The man looked at him and shrugged. 'I have my orders.'

The Doctor stood up. 'Then you have your answer as to whether we can work together. Get out. Get out now!'

He approached the man, who stood up. He was huge.

'I wonder if you'll talk easier than Ji Woo would,' he mused. He looked at Donna. 'I bet *she* would.'

'I wouldn't!' said Donna, her chin jutting out. 'I would,' she hissed *sotto voce* to the Doctor. 'You have to know that I would absolutely tell anyone anything under torture. Like, anything.'

'That's fine,' said the Doctor.

'So if you were thinking, maybe she can have a little bit of torture whilst I think of a clever thing to get us out of this, I absolutely need to tell you that no, even a little bit of torture will not be all right.'

He smiled. 'Yeah I get it, Donna.' He straightened up to the man. 'I really suggest you leave now.'

'I'm just here,' said the man. 'On public property. It's my perfect right to be here.'

'*Journalists!*' said the Doctor. 'It's our cabin. You don't have any right to be in here at all!'

The man tapped underneath his shirt. There was the outline of a gun holster. 'Oh, I have "rights".'

They stood there, glaring at each other. The neighbouring cabins had finally realised something was happening, and had come out, yawning and in nightshirts, to see what was going on.

'Go back to bed, it's nothing,' the Doctor told them.

'He's got a gun!' screamed one woman in Portuguese, staring at the huge man.

'Why's he wearing those sunglasses?' said another. 'And the earpiece!'

The huge man slowly turned his head to face the person who had spoken. Someone else made a noise.

The steward from the end of the carriage emerged, looking anxious. 'Sir? Sir, I must ask everyone to return to—'

'But he's got a gun!'

Everyone started clamouring and shouting and trying to push their way past in the narrow corridor, except they were going both ways and there wasn't enough room. People started to panic. The man thrust his way through the now very crowded, very narrow corridor, the Doctor pursuing him.

When he got to the end, the man simply shoved the short steward, who had bravely stood in front of him, out of the way. Immediately the smaller man fell heavily against the side door, banging his head on the glass with a sickening sound, and sliding gracelessly down to the ground.

His colleague, a young girl in a white shirt and black skirt, saw this happen and began to scream and run towards the front of the train, jumping at the man's arm to try and grab his gun. The man shook her off with horrible force, and ran through the adjoining carriage towards the front of the train, with the Doctor in hot pursuit.

Between the carriages, the wind blew fiercely and the noise was incredible as the train shot on, into a dawn they could now see rising over the dramatically beautiful mountains. The carriages bounced over the track.

The Doctor looked at the man. He wasn't remotely concerned, simply picking his way over the coupling as if walking through a field. He touched his earpiece again.

'Aha,' said the Doctor. 'Ah! Why didn't I realise? I am so *thick*! Of course I know who you are…' He shook his head. 'Who else would you send? Oi!' he shouted. 'I know you!'

The man didn't even turn round. They were in the very front carriage of the train, which meant the only place to go was the main steam engine at the front, that gave the train its special status as one of the great rail journeys of the world. He pulled the handle and fell into the engine room, the Doctor grabbing it behind him and tumbling back in.

'How are the sound fields of Cadmia this time of year…?' the Doctor was yelling.

The engine room was open to the elements. A large man, covered in soot, stood looking at them. Beyond him was the driver's panel itself. The driver turned round, anxiously. The Doctor was conscious that he looked out of breath and dishevelled, whereas the other man looked exactly as he had before.

'I'm security,' said the man, with his usual calm, touching his earpiece. 'This person here is an escaped fugitive. Help me seize him!'

'Yes, and like all escaped fugitives I take a lot of long luxurious steam train excursions,' said the Doctor, aware he sounded frenzied and overexcited. 'Quick, please, help me disarm this man. He's incredibly dangerous.'

The engineer and the driver looked at one another anxiously, clearly doubting who to trust.

They hesitated only for a split second, but it was all the Doctor needed. He raised his elbow, and with one swift movement knocked off the other man's dark wraparound sunglasses.

Chapter
Twenty-Three

This was, in retrospect, a terrible mistake.

Chapter
Twenty-Four

The man's strange, owl-like yellow eyes took in the carriage, blinking. The engineer picked up his spade and went for him, as if a spider had just crawled in. But the train driver's reaction was worse: his head twisted right round, he inadvertently took his hand off the dead man's handle, just as his foot instinctively pressed harder on the accelerator in fright.

The ancient engines made the most appalling noise as they tried to do two things at once. The driver, with a look of utter horror on his face and still unable to tear his eyes away from the yellow-eyed man, tried to push the handle back, but it swung uselessly, completely unable to connect with a train that was now bucking forwards like a runaway horse.

The engineer came at the yellow-eyed man with a hammer. It didn't affect him in the slightest. Instead, the man slowly but inexorably moved against him, pushing the engineer towards the open side of the train, without apparent exertion.

'Enough of that,' said the Doctor, his eyes searching the train controls. He had seen already what was coming; and knew that they were powerless to stop it. He leapt to the front of the train and swung the handle but it could not engage; instead, he made the engine lurch to the left, quickly landing the engineer on top of the man.

The train bounced, one, two, three times. It was speeding up down the track.

And like a tiny dot in the distance of the encroaching dawn, the Doctor could just see the infamously tall and beautiful Viaduct 13, stretching 150 metres in the air, terrifyingly high and thin. Far away… but getting closer every second.

There was absolutely no way the runaway train could hold on.

'Move,' the Doctor shouted at the startled driver. Then he hauled both the man and the engineer up from the floor. The noise level was terrific; the train was chattering their teeth.

'Stop it you two.' He grabbed the man's gun and hurled it over the side of the train. It took a very long time to fall, as they rattled on. 'We have to save this train.'

He opened the connecting doors and ushered them all, engineer and driver too, back across the narrow divide – louder and more rattling than ever – and back through into the main set of carriages. Six volunteers came forwards and held the man with the yellow eyes back. As ever, he seemed completely unperturbed as to the turn of events.

Donna pushed her way forwards in her pyjamas. 'What's going on?' she asked nervously.

The Doctor stared at her. '"Let's not take the TARDIS," you said. "People like coffee," you said. "Let's travel the world," you said!'

Donna wasn't listening: she was staring at the man. 'Oh no, look at him! Was he an alien all along? When did you realise?'

'Oh, ages ago,' lied the Doctor. 'Come on, everyone, back. Back!'

The Doctor glanced at the people standing there, then leaned out of the window. There was a steep drop below. The rising sun was shining strongly against the mountain side. The train bounced again, once, twice again, always faster, plummeting down the mountainside as people shouted and shrunk back.

'What are you thinking? Parachutes?' said Donna.

'Rarely carried on trains.'

'What if everybody took their bedsheets...'

A boulder shook itself free from the side of the track of the banging train and tumbled down the mountainside. It was an extraordinarily long way down.

The Doctor shook his head. 'OK, everyone,' he said. 'Keep going back. Back.' He ushered them away from the engine side. 'Come on, come on.'

The passengers moved quickly to the back compartment of the train, silent and terrified. Many of them were elderly.

'Can you stop it?' said Donna.

The Doctor's mouth was a thin line. 'I don't know. Move, everyone! You too, Donna. *Move!* Back of the train!'

The Doctor turned in the wooden corridor. They could hear glasses and bottles were falling from the bar, smashing up and down the train. It was bouncing higher and higher now, as if any moment would be its last one on the rails.

'Come on, Doctor! Let's see what we can do,' said Donna, worried.

The Doctor ran back to the front of the train, with Donna right behind him. Then, just before he crossed the windy door to the engine, he turned round promptly, gave her a grin, and winked at the man with the yellow eyes.

'I know you. I know all about you. And all I'm telling you, is that we need Donna, OK? We won't get there without her. Do you see the logic in that? Do you see the sense in it? You need us. I need you. Hold her. *Capisce?* Ooh. *Capisce.* I like it. *Capisce?'*

The man shook off the people holding him and nodded, as if he were completely unconcerned – and, with a push, the Doctor sent Donna backwards into his arms.

'What?' she shouted, wriggling frantically. 'Don't leave me with this maniac!'

'Sorry,' said the Doctor. 'Sometimes, the situation requires a maniac.'

And he slammed shut the door of the carriage, and headed alone back to the engine.

'Wait for me!' shouted Donna, kicking and struggling in the man's arms. 'Let me go! I need to help the Doctor!'

'Yeah, in a minute,' said the man, still sounding blithely unconcerned.

'I mean, it, get your hands off me!' said Donna in a tone of voice that would have given most people pause. The man did not move.

In the next instant she'd bitten his hand. Again, people would have jumped at that. The man simply tugged down, as if brushing off a fly. Next, Donna butted her head straight up. It connected – it would have hurt, surely. But the man showed no sign of pain whatsoever; he did not change his stance. She did it again. Again, no pain response.

'What are you?' she breathed.

'I'll tell you when we get to the back of the train,' he grunted, dragging her across the connecting link of the great bouncing train into the rear carriages.

And then there was a terrible, terrible crashing noise.

Chapter
Twenty-Five

They froze. The other passengers started to yell. The man unfolded his glasses rapidly back on his face, and started pulling on Donna again. They ran back and back as the front of the train catapulted itself up, up in the air, everything beginning to slide down to the back.

Donna held on to the side with a panicky feeling in her stomach. She could feel it: the shift in the air as the wheels left the track. For a moment, they were floating. Everything fell still and very, very slow.

She stared outside at the great beautiful mountains beyond, shimmering in the pink of the early morning, feeling two things simultaneously; the oddest sense of being inside and outside herself looking in; so that even through the fear and panic she could hear herself thinking, 'So. This is it girl. This is where it ends. This is where you'll crash down. I wonder if they'll find you? How will Gramps cope? How will he manage? Hopefully I won't be too burned to get home. I wish… I wish the Doctor was here. I wish I could be holding his hand. That would…'

A memory suddenly flashed across her mind: a day not long before when the Doctor had made a quick side trip to a planet called Lafayette. She had not been allowed to go with him, and he hadn't been long. When she'd asked, he'd merely said he was visiting somebody in hospital. She wondered now. She knew it was an old friend. She didn't ask the prognosis.

He had been so sad afterwards, she'd had to tell him about the time she and Hettie had gone out with their skirts tucked into their knickers deliberately for a dare to see who would bother to let them know and nobody had cared except for a dog who'd followed them all the way in case they had sausages and they'd ended up buying him a sausage so at least *somebody* had a good day, and he'd finally thrown his head back and laughed, then he'd looked at her and said, 'Oh, it is *so* much better for me when you're here, Donna.'

And she hadn't thought of it again until now: but now, she wondered.

When the hour came.

Did he?

And all of that ran straight through her head, in the short milliseconds it took, as the great locomotive's front went up in the air, and down, down, down, and the entire train held its breath to see where it would land.

There was a great screeching and a screaming noise and sparks went up from the metal undercarriage of the train as it banged down again, once, twice. The noise of twisted metal was terrific.

Suddenly, there was a clang and, incredibly, the wheels found the tracks, found the groove. They bounced back down again, but they were still on the rails, still moving. As they hit a flat stretch of track, though, they were slowing, definitely slowing; the forward momentum had gone, had been dissipated.

Finally, with a smell of burning from the tracks, they stopped. He'd done it. The Doctor had saved the train.

Donna pulled away from the man and ran up to the front of the carriages to open the connecting door. But as she did so, the wind whipped in, and she saw to her horror that she was staring out onto the rail ahead: into empty space.

There was no engine there. The front of the train had gone.

They had been uncoupled, and she could see they had come to a stop just on the long flat run up to the massive viaduct shining in the distance. And, far ahead of her now, still speeding up, was the engine, flying faster and faster, completely out of control and completely unstoppable.

'No!' she shouted, but the sound of her voice was whipped away on the heavy, scented wind.

Chapter
Twenty-Six

The Doctor was attempting to consider his options, at some speed.

There was no stopping 400 tonnes of rocketing engine with a screwdriver. He would make, perhaps, the bridge, without the dooming physics of the swinging tail of the train behind him – but beyond that was a town. A station, and a town – it would be an utter catastrophe. He had to stop it.

The bridge was approaching at punishing speed as the engine bucked and jumped. He glanced around. What had Donna said? That idea of hers that he'd ridiculed? Sure enough, there was a pile of old oilskins in the corner, presumably for the crewmen when it rained. There was a reason they called it the rainforest.

He looked at the handles on the train once again. Would it accelerate more? He started filling up the engine with coke, and pushed it to its full extent. It didn't feel like the train could move any faster, but it did.

The Doctor grabbed the sheets. Then, with some effort, he moved every piece of machinery and bag of fuel to the left hand side of the train. He used his screwdriver to unfasten anything attached to the wall, and piled it all up on the other side. Sure enough, the engine started to list.

The train was now unimaginably fast. Good. It had to be. It couldn't stay on the rails now. It had to come off. It had to stop, before it met an immoveable object in its way.

The train rocked dangerously now. The glorious, impossibly beautiful Viaduct 13 was dead ahead.

Carefully, keeping an eye on its undulations, the Doctor climbed up through the window and pulled himself up onto the roof of the carriage. Here the wind was incredible; he practically had to surf to stay upright. Beneath him was the viaduct, plunging down unimaginably deep into the canyon below. He let the wind roar through him, briefly closing his eyes.

The morning sun felt huge and bright and close overhead. Even though it couldn't have much effect, he shifted his weight slightly from one side to the other, over on the left hand side to try and help it. The wheels were already lifting, just a bit, a tiny bit… and here came the bridge, here it came ahead…

BANG. They hit the first stone stanchion at full pelt, and the train lifted to the left, just a little, and BANG another one, and the Doctor felt the great magnificent engine beneath him, the welded mass of pistons and coils and pure power, lift up, finally, to the left. Once it had begun to tilt, gravity did the rest. It banged down again once, twice – but the third time it could no longer overcome its physical destiny. The train took off into mid-air, just as the Doctor dived over the right-hand side, leaping outwards as far as he could, holding the oil sheets up in the air, and hoping for the best.

For an instant they were both flying, the great engine plunging down. The Doctor's descent slowed – but was it slowing enough? Was it nearly enough? To crash in the ravine below? He didn't look, instead following his own mantra, the mantra of his life: don't look down. Because he knew his descent was too fast. Far too fast.

And, as he cut through the air, all the things that fall pulsed through his head: a glorious downed pheasant on the wing; and a windfall apple in Lincolnshire; and a golden ball in Pisa; and a hammer and a feather on the moon; and a wall in the bitter east; and every passing snowflake and lonely airman and oh so many tumbling stars…

And he felt a part of all of these things.

The noise the train made crashing into the ravine made the mountains tremble.

Donna, watching a very small dot from several kilometres away – it took the sound a short time to reach her – stifled a horrified sob.

The Doctor, still falling, closed his eyes… and suddenly found, WHOOSH, a huge fireball erupting below him sent a mass of heat up into the air, lifting the oil sheet and blowing him far over, taking him upwards, lessening the deadly speed of his plummet. He opened his eyes and looked up at the bright pink sky in surprise and gratitude.

This quickly turned to action as he realised he had to plan his descent so as not to fall straight on top of the burning engine, which was already scorching the trees around it and looked set fair to cause a major conflagration.

He aimed, instead, for the pounding river that ran beneath the viaduct – the reason for its existence – and plunged deep into its mysterious waters. He let himself sink, as billowing black smoke from the engine filled the air above, making it thick and hard to breathe. He let himself drift downwards into ever darker water, surrounded by the strange animals of this deep jungle, who came to inspect this new intruder in their world. They coiled around him, and swam by in curiosity as he spun and tumbled deep in the water, patiently waiting for a while for the smoke to clear, then he left them behind.

He broke the surface of the water, as he burst through it into the sweet morning air, the pink sky reflecting off the water, a smile on his face.

Chapter
Twenty-Seven

It was a bright new morning. The passengers and crew of the train got a little bonfire going in a clearing and were warming themselves on it waiting for rescue.

They'd all heard the explosion, seen the train going down and heard the great WHOOMPH from the exploding boilers. People were muttering about the Doctor's extraordinary self-sacrifice in uncoupling the engine from the rest of the train. The stewards were dazedly making tea for everyone; maintaining, even now, their immaculate standards. There was nothing to do except sit and wait for rescue.

Donna sat apart, glaring at the man with the yellow eyes, whose fault all of this was – and who appeared to be completely untroubled by any of it.

Donna stood up. 'Right, I'll be off. Thanks for the tea,' she said.

The man stood up too. 'I'm coming.'

'No you're not.' She glanced at the others. 'Hold him back, he's dangerous!'

The man didn't say anything as the stewards and the rest of the passengers on board piled in and led him back to the train, locking him in one of the bathrooms.

He watched through the window as Donna launched herself determinedly into the thick Brazilian rainforest, an environment for which she was supremely ill-equipped and badly dressed. Then he simply smashed through the door, pulled some bottles of water out from under the mess and broken glass of the restaurant car, dropped lightly off the other side of the train, and took off quietly to follow her.

Donna was having an argument with herself. It went like this: she'd seen him get out of a lot of things, right? That was how it worked. When she was with him, there was nothing they couldn't do. He always managed it.

But there was the little voice in her head. She hadn't been with him then. Not at all. She hadn't been there. Not at the end. Not when she thought he might have needed her. Not in the way she'd have needed him.

It was unbearable to think that way. But she kept seeing it in her head, over and over again, the tiny dot that was the train engine, watching it career along the great viaduct, bounce, tip and finally fall, sparking a massive explosion. She'd seen it all.

Still. Surely there was a chance. Surely.

The light fell through the thick green canopy ahead, and it wasn't hard, at first, to see the great plume of smoke she was heading for. All she had to do was keep marching towards it. That was all she was going to think about. As to what she would find when she got there, who knew?

But as she got further into the jungle, she started to worry. Firstly, the sun, from the cool of the early dawn, had turned punishingly hot and steamy. Condensation evaporated from her pyjamas. That was another thing she should have probably thought through, Donna realised as she continued. She was wearing her pyjamas. At least she had her shoes on. But she had stormed out of camp without another thought in her head apart from getting away from the alien, and finding the Doctor. The luxury of the air-conditioned train carriages, with their comfortable seats and waiter service, had lulled her into a totally false sense of security. This wasn't a little jaunt in the English countryside; she wasn't going to cross a stile and find a little café selling bacon sandwiches and local cheese.

This was the Brazilian rainforest. One of the most hostile environments on Earth. And the deeper she went in, the thicker the canopy overhead became, and the less of a fix she had on the column of smoke she was heading for, without the faintest knowledge of what she'd find when she got there.

Donna tried not to think about how stupid she'd been. She turned round to look at the way back, but it was simply a thick layer of plant and foliage coverage that looked exactly the same whichever way. She glanced up at the sky. The sun was… OK. If the sun rose in the east… Hang on, did the sun rise in the east in the southern hemisphere?

'Geography!' she thought again to herself crossly. Blooming geography with its colouring in and oxbow lakes and the way her teacher hadn't bothered if she'd read *Smash Hits* at the back of the class. It was their fault, really.

She tried to quell her mounting panic and take stock. OK. Let's say that the sun was in the east. In that case the smoke was coming north west. North north west. She felt quite pleased with herself for remembering that. It sounded like a film. OK. If she kept heading north north west, then she would get there, or at least she'd get near the wreckage. Surely it would have scattered quite far? And then maybe she would…

All she wanted, she realised, was for him to appear, grinning, through the trees ahead. Anything else she couldn't allow to cross her mind.

Well, she told herself sternly. He might be trapped. He might need help. He certainly needed her, and she was perfectly capable of getting there under her own steam. Right. North north west. And water. She definitely needed water. She looked around.

It was boiling hot and she'd discarded the blanket she'd had wrapped around her outside the train. Her light cotton pyjamas weren't doing a very good job of protecting her fair skin from the sun, but it was fairly easy to stay in the shade of the heavy trees. Donna's only problem was wondering what else was sheltering from the sun in the shade of the heavy trees. Already she could feel the little *pique pique* stinging of something on her exposed ankles.

Continuing in as straight a line as she could manage, she came to a wide, murky stream with a dangerous-looking current. It didn't seem to narrow, as far as she could see, either up or down.

'Right, Donna Noble,' she said to herself, out loud.

The jungle was a noisier place than she'd realised. It was full of creatures chuttering and tweetering to themselves, calling across the canopies of vines. Birds of extraordinary foliage and colours flew across the tops of the trees, but Donna was too worried about what was writhing beneath her feet to pay them much attention.

She spoke out loud to convince herself that everything was fine. It was just a park with slightly larger animals, that was all.

'And also, everyone's hunted all the really scary animals to extinction,' she said, again out loud. 'A bunch of horrible American dentists has probably made my life a lot easier. Yeah.'

She knelt down on the thick rotting vegetation by the side of the water to take a drink. It would be all right, wouldn't it? I mean, animals drank out of it, didn't they?

And she was getting so horribly thirsty and dizzy. She had moved far too fast to begin with; she had pushed herself through high vines and climbed over tree trunks with reckless abandon in her fever to find the Doctor. But in this incredible heat... How could anyone move in this?

She knelt down, feeling exposed in the break in the jungle cover. The sun beat harder than ever on her exposed neck and she tried to pull up the collar of her pyjamas to cover it. The river was full of weeds and old logs floating downstream. She leaned in to scoop up some water…

'Stop!'

A voice! And there was a thundering crashing sound through the trees. She looked up, startled, hopeful and frightened, all at the same time.

Standing there behind her in the clearing was the man with the yellow eyes.

Donna jumped up. 'Get away from me,' she said, glancing around. There was a large, hard fruit down by her feet. She picked it up. 'Or I'll throw this at you.'

The man looked at her, his glasses back on, his earpiece in place. His face was inscrutable, his body language, as ever, extremely calm. 'You do that,' he said, seemingly unconcerned.

Donna hurled it at him. It was heavier than it looked; like a bowling ball. She got it nowhere near him.

'Right, can we talk now?' he said.

Donna glanced around for another. 'You stay away!' She stepped backwards, starting to splash in the water.

'Stop!' he said and this time, unusually, moved quickly. He grabbed at her arm, just as what Donna had taken for a dead log floating downstream leapt out of the water at incredible speed, opened its jaws and let them crash down shut exactly where her arm had been merely seconds before.

'Argh!' Donna screamed and leapt backwards as the crocodile flailed its great head around, desperately searching the source of its prey. It thrashed its tail and started to run out of the water onto the bank.

The man sighed, as if he'd briefly mislaid his car keys. 'Quick,' he said, and swung himself up to the lowest branch of the nearest tree with ease.

Donna blinked at him.

'Come on!' he said.

The crocodile was running up the bank, raising its head blindly to try and stumble onto what it was searching for. Its huge jaws once again closed on thin air.

Donna didn't need to be told twice. With a feat of agility that would have surprised her weary gym teacher, she grabbed the man's outstretched arm, and swung herself up onto the same branch. The beast found the tree and ran around it. Donna stared at it. It looked like something from the prehistoric era; a relic, a pet of the dinosaurs they had forgotten and left behind. It was fascinating in its way.

'What do we do now?' she said.

'We wait for it to get tired of us,' said the man with the yellow eyes. 'Or we start throwing coconuts down on it. Mind you, given your aim we may just have to wait for it to grow old and die. Here.' He handed her a large bottle of water.

Donna looked at it suspiciously. 'What's this?'

'It's sealed,' said the man quickly as if he was expecting her objection.

Donna took a long pull. She hadn't realised how thirsty she was; even warm, the water tasted fantastic. Then she stopped and they sat there awkwardly.

'So, do you run into the jungle often?' the man said in a companionable tone of voice.

There was a long pause, punctuated only with the scuttling of the crocodile down below.

'What's wrong with your eyes?' she said eventually.

'Well, nothing,' said the man. 'But you knew that, I think.'

Donna paused for a while. 'So you... you're... Where are you from, then?'

'You wouldn't have heard of it,' said the man.

'Try me,' said Donna. 'I've been further than you think.'

'Cadmia,' said the man. 'Lower cycle of what you call GJ504 and we call Cadmia.'

Donna nodded.

'So,' said the man. 'Me being alien not a surprise?'

'Not really,' said Donna. 'Most people I meet are.'

'But you're local.'

'To here?'

There was a pause as Donna watched, amazed, as four flamingos delicately wandered down to the river and started dipping their heads daintily. The crocodile went crazy, charged after them then charged back as they elegantly fled, then returned to its sentry post.

'It doesn't feel like I am,' she admitted. 'But, theoretically, yeah. I'm from Earth.'

'It's nice,' said the man.

'Why are you here?' said Donna. 'Bad stuff? Are you just like the bad guy they hire when they need bad stuff doing? Do you get, like, a visa? Like if you can do bad stuff worse than anyone on Earth can do, you get a special work visa?'

The man tilted his head. 'I'm… useful in certain situations.'

'Because of all the torturing?'

'No.' He shrugged mildly. 'I have no idea why you humans like it so much. On Cadmia, it simply wouldn't cross our minds.'

'But you know it's wrong.'

He took off his glasses to polish them. 'Is it?'

'Seriously, you don't know it's wrong?'

The man shook his head. 'Well, my first job was in a vivisection lab, so I just assumed that all the species on this planet cut each other up for fun from time to time. I mean, there's no violence on Cadmia…'

'None at all?'

The man shrugged. 'How would there be?'

'What happens when people get angry with each other?'

The man shrugged again. 'We don't. I mean, I didn't actually understand what the word meant before I started travelling.'

'There's no war? No fighting?'

The man shook his head. 'There's no peril at all. I have… we've evolved out of an adrenal response. We're an agrarian vegetarian society. I don't… I mean, there's nothing to fear on Cadmia. Nothing at all.'

'So you don't get scared of anything?' She looked at him shrewdly. 'That's why you weren't scared on the train! You can't get scared... Can you get angry?'

The man shook his head. 'Well, anger is just fear. Externalised. You knew that, yes?'

Donna blinked. 'Is it? Oh, I suppose it is. So. No, then.'

'No,' said the man mildly.

'So if you needed someone to solve a problem people had with getting angry...'

The man nodded. 'Oh, we're in demand all over the galaxy.'

'But you must be scared of dying.'

'Why?' said the man. 'What's the point? We simply go back to the land and fertilise it. We come from the land and go back to the land and everyone is nourished by the land. What's to be scared of in that?'

Donna leaned in fascinated. 'No war... Do you have love affairs? Art? Music?'

'We have. We have sounds...' said the man.

'Sounds. That's it? No Beatles? No David Bowie?'

'I don't understand.'

'So why aren't you back on your perfect paradise, then?'

'Drought,' he said. 'So, some of us... we take jobs away from home. We send back money, and we can make rain and so on, and we carry on.'

'Hasn't anyone ever invaded you?'

'Everyone is welcome to Cadmia,' said the man. 'Hardly anyone stays.'

'I'm not surprised: your nightclubs must be awful,' agreed Donna. 'What's your name? Have you got one, or have you evolved out of that too?'

'Fief.'

'I'm not going to say pleased to meet you,' said Donna severely, 'because you're an extremely bad guy.'

The man didn't say anything for a while after that. The crocodile was continuing to circle the bottom of the tree warily, unwilling to let its supper get away.

'The other man,' said Fief.

'Mmm.'

'He's an alien too?'

'How'd you guess?'

'His eyes are strange.'

Donna looked at him, and grinned, but he didn't notice and went on.

'What is he?'

'Why should I tell you?'

'No reason, I don't mind.'

'Well. He's a Time Lord,' said Donna, quite smugly.

There was a very long pause. The crocodile snapped on.

'A Time Lord?' The timbre of his voice didn't change, but Donna reckoned if it could, it would have sounded impressed. 'An ancient relic of the long-dead infamous archaic species from Gallifrey?'

'That's him. Give or take some hair gel.' Donna gave him a look. 'Good luck by the way if you're planning to kidnap or torture *him*.'

The Cadmian shook his head. 'No,' he said. He looked out over the canopy of trees. 'You understand.

I do not have a fear response. But I recognise it in the many, many species that do. The man from Gallifrey. He provokes a fear response.'

'Nah, he's all right,' said Donna.

'He provokes fear. And anger. But not in you. How curious.'

'Maybe I'm extremely brave,' said Donna.

'You must be,' said the man. 'Otherwise you would not spend so much time with someone who imperils you so.'

They sat for a while longer.

'Although I do wonder what you were doing before that was so much worse than this.'

'Temping,' said Donna.

'I see,' said the man.

Donna drank a little more water and felt more herself again, the dizziness gone. 'I have to go and find him now,' she said.

They both looked down at the crocodile, who continued to stalk them, his tail waving lazily. With one easy movement, all the more chilling because he made it look like he was simply returning an errant tennis ball, Fief grabbed a hard-shelled unripe fruit and aimed it straight at the animal's eye.

The beast dropped like a stone.

'Is he going to be all right?' said Donna, who was finding getting out of the tree a rather more graceless process than vaulting up it. 'Ouch. Let me go first.' She tore her pyjamas and swore. 'Right, now you have to walk in front of me.' She looked at the unconscious beast. 'Seriously, though. I know he was trying to eat us and everything, but is he going to be all right?'

Fief stared at her.

'What?'

'I don't... I'm sorry, I don't understand the question,' he said.

'Is he going to recover?'

'I don't know,' said Fief. 'Why would you ask that?'

'Because I'm worried about it.'

'But would it change your behaviour?'

Donna thought about it. 'No. I need to find the Doctor, not open a croc hospital.'

The man nodded. 'Well then.' He started to lead on back to the river.

'You're actually quite zen for a cold-blooded killer,' said Donna, stumbling along behind him.

Fief did not turn round but simply passed back the water bottle. Donna took another long draw then watched as, without apparent effort, Fief lifted up an enormous log lying on the bank and set it firmly across the perilous river crossing. He stood up lightly and walked across it.

'Um,' she said, edging along carefully and trying to keep both her nerve and her balance. 'Erm... Can I just ask at which point in this process you're planning to kill me?'

Fief turned back towards her. She realised with a shock he had removed his glasses once again, obviously no longer feeling the need for them. His eyes were the yellow of an owl's. They took away all notion of humanity from him. It was very peculiar.

'Why would I do that?' he said. 'You lead me to where this disease is originating. We eradicate it. Our work is done. My employer will be satisfied. It seems to me you would be more help than hindrance.'

Donna was briefly flattered by the compliment. 'But can you stop torture or hurting other people?' she shouted after him as he lightly reached the end of the log. She was still inching across it.

'Like the crocodile?' he said.

'Um, yeah. From now on, then,' said Donna, feeling guilty.

Fief looked at her, then turned to carry onwards. He promised nothing.

Chapter
Twenty-Eight

Deep in the beautiful colonial offices of the Ice Palace, there was movement. A reckoning.

He sat back with a satisfied grin. The casualties were mounting. But that simply meant more money, pouring in. All very satisfactory.

He looked at the news screens. Aha! It had hit the teenagers. Those noisy, gobby, angry teenagers, always on their phones. A perfect breeding ground for internalised discontent: furious, entitled, and completely impotent to change anything. Perfect.

He watched the blue shining manhole cover pulse and pulse, the billions of little Rempaths obediently sucked up through the high-speed network from the blood of the lost... all ready for transfer.

Then he caught some other chatter on the channels and frowned. The Korean operation was compromised, he knew... but when he reviewed the footage of how it had happened, he rose up in a rage.

*

Wilf was in the wrong place at the wrong time, which when you had lived as long as he had was bound to happen sooner or later.

It turned out to be the bottom deck of the number 190. Up Chiswick High road, on the way to exchange his library books. Couldn't have been a more ordinary day. He was considering a bun. One of those twirly ones with icing and raisins. And maybe a cup of tea. Cup of tea. Bun. With his new books. This sounded like an excellent plan. He'd go to the Hot House café, where sometimes his old friend Al stopped by. That would be even nicer.

It might be a wet rainy day, but Wilf was on a warm bus with a pleasant morning ahead, as long as he remembered Sylvia's kale she'd asked for. He didn't know what kale was and he had the strongest suspicion she didn't either, but she'd asked him and he'd promised and therefore he'd be strongly advised to get on it.

At first it was nothing, just a quiet 'Excuse me'. A lady was getting on the bus with a large buggy and a toddler whinging at her heels. She looked exhausted, beyond harassed. Her braids escaped her beanie hat; there was food on her jacket that might have been there for a while. The little one was whining constantly and the huge buggy was proving extremely difficult to manoeuvre in the small space.

The bus driver, a man, was unsympathetic as the woman struggled to find her oyster card. Wilf stood up to offer his seat but she shot him a fierce look and shook her head, as if he'd offered to steal one of her children. There was some tutting up the back from a noisy group of teenagers. Wilf had learned to tune out teenagers. There'd always been noisy teenagers.

In his day, the local battle-axe, Mrs MacCrorie, who had one gigantic bosom and a loud booming voice and ran the local greengrocers with an iron fist, would simply have told them to pipe down or she would tell their mothers, and they would meekly listen and quieten down, at least till she was out of sight. These days, though, nobody dared to tell teenagers anything. They were all precious little darlings, he supposed. Told they were incredibly special little flowers from the day they were born by their doting mums and dads; bought the latest of everything; gifted entitlement. Which apparently meant that nobody had to wear headphones any more and could play their favourite music in public wherever they wanted.

Wilf hadn't minded age-related deafness at all.

The woman had inched, bright red from embarrassment, to the middle of the bus to put the buggy out of the way. The teenagers had been jumping all over the seats, taking over half of them in their puppyish ebullience, shouting obscenities at one another. The woman had to stand. The baby started to wail. Meanwhile the toddler was watching the big boys and girls with wide eyes. Every time there was a particularly nasty swear word the mother winced and the child's mouth gaped open. Wilf sighed. He hadn't served in a war for nothing, he thought. They hadn't fought for this.

Now the teenagers had found an incredibly rude music video and were playing it at top volume, screaming along the words about violence and drugs. One of the boys showed the X-rated video to the little boy, to peals of nasty laughter. The bus driver moved on, refusing to turn his head.

Wilf sighed once more and got up. 'Leave the little boy alone,' he said. 'Put that off and sit down.'

The chief boy stood up, sniggering at his fellows. He was enormous, Wilf thought. Huge and beefy and far too fat for a boy still wearing school uniform. He should be running about a field with his friends, Wilf thought belatedly. Or even marching up and down a parade ground. The boy had a blond quiff and some angry red spots around his Adam's apple. His skin was red and puffy, like a rotting fruit about to burst and he smelled overwhelmingly of cheap aftershave, as if he'd emptied a bottle on top of himself. He clutched his large electronic device close to him, waving it menacingly. The tinny gangster music resounded from the speakers.

'Are you going to make me?'

Wilf looked up and down the bus. The young mother was desperately hanging her head as the baby continued to scream, obviously wishing herself anywhere else. There were two old ladies also sitting on the bus, but both of them instantly fixed their eyes looking outside the window as if absolutely nothing was happening and they could comfortably ignore it. And the bus driver drove on.

'I guess I'll have to,' said Wilf, making a swipe for it.

More by chance than skill he reached out to take it from him, caught it on the side, then fumbled and lost it again; in the process he sent it whizzing against the side of the bus's metal pole. The screen cracked audibly and the music stopped. There was a terrible silence in the bus. The boy's face, once it took in what had actually happened, turned puce.

Suddenly he was terrifying. He loomed over Wilf, his beefy bulk overshadowing the older man completely. He lifted up a hand.

'I'm going to do you for that,' he said. 'Come on, boys.'

His buddies moved forward, gleeful at the battle on their hands; an excuse to vent their anger.

'Now lads,' said Wilf, his voice quavering, annoyingly. 'You know that was an accident.'

'Ain't no accidents,' said the chief boy in a menacing voice. 'We all saw what you done. We know our rights. That was my property, mate. And you're going to pay.'

The woman with the children stifled a sob. The boy raised his arm. His face changed briefly – as if a stab of something had gone through him. He grimaced. And then he brought down his fist.

Chapter
Twenty-Nine

'I'm so hungry.'

They'd been marching for what felt like hours, and they were still, it seemed, no closer to the pluming smoke in the forest in front of them. The shadowy bits of the rainforest were steamy and ridiculously hot, and Donna's pyjamas were wringing wet. She'd ceased caring.

Fief was wearing the same blue shirt and dark trousers he'd been wearing when she'd met him for the first time at the internet troll's house. She realised belatedly that they probably *were* the same: he probably didn't sweat the same way humans did. What a funny species he was.

'Is there nothing to eat? Can't you catch a fish?'

Fief regarded her again with that level yellow-eyed gaze. 'But you said not to harm anything.'

Donna sighed. 'OK, except for fish. I probably didn't mean fish.'

'And crocodiles.'

'You must be so much fun at parties. Do Cadmians have parties?'

'We celebrate our unity and oneness,' said Fief.

'Is it fun?'

Fief was completely puzzled by the question.

'I don't think being a Cadmian is remotely fun,' said Donna.

'Yes, your species seems much happier,' returned Fief serenely. 'Now. Fish.'

'Actually, I think I just saw some bananas,' said Donna.

In fact they were plantain, and they cooked beautifully over a small fire Fief built. Then they headed on.

As long as Donna didn't have to think of anything but putting one foot in front of the other, and feel like she was moving forwards, then it wasn't too bad. She was doing something. She was going to find the Doctor. It was fine.

As soon as she thought about whether or not he'd survived the fall, or what was going on out in the world where the Rempaths were running rampant, her brain clouded over. So she stopped concentrating on anything like that. She had always had the knack for not thinking about things that made her feel uncomfortable, and she used it now.

She kept her eye open for snakes and scorpions, and tried not to think about how many bites she was getting on her ankles. Eventually however, when they sat down for a brief rest (she needed them: Fief didn't appear to), it was too much for her, and she scratched her delicate skin hard.

'Rrrraaaaah,' she said.

'What are you doing?'

'Scratching an itch. It's so infuriating but so satisfying at the same time.'

'An itch?'

'Don't tell me. Cadmians don't itch.'

'Is it irritating?'

'Yes. What do you do when things are irritating?'

In response Fief pulled up his trouser leg. His sallow skin was completely covered all over with the tiny angry little bites. 'We endure.'

Donna stared at him. 'Seriously. They don't itch?'

'How could it upset me? They simply are.'

He cast around, and found an aloe plant, which he squeezed into another leaf with his bare hands.

'Here,' he said, dabbing it gently on Donna's bites with his huge hand. It stung at first, then a strange and delicious coolness started to settle on her skin.

'Oh, that is so much better,' said Donna, closing her eyes.

'I believe this is supposed to ameliorate the sting of Earth insects.' He smiled wryly. 'Our training is quite thorough.' He threw the rest of the leaf away.

Donna looked at him, astonished. 'But what about you?' she said. 'Don't you want some?'

'It is not necessary,' said Fief.

Donna found herself smiling. 'You are so strange.'

*

The evening scents were beginning to settle towards the end of the day; thick heavy bougainvillea growing wild, its heavy trails everywhere; deep red flowers beginning to curl up for the night; a heavy scent of orchids on the air – when Fief halted her, and she stood stock still.

'Hush,' he said.

'What is it?' whispered Donna, looking carefully up into the trees. The twilight was settling, and her eyes persisted in seeing every vine a snake, every log a crocodile, every ant something poisonous, every glint in the woods behind them sharp teeth watching. Waiting.

'I hear something.'

Donna couldn't hear anything at first. Just the usual cawing of the birds exchanging their farewells; a far-distant – thankfully – honking which might have been wild pig or rhinoceros. A flock of brightly coloured cockatoos took off from a distant tree, disappearing into the bright purple evening like a picture from a child's story book.

'It is so beautiful here,' said Donna.

'It is?' said Fief, unconcerned. 'Ssh.'

Sure enough, now Donna too could hear a rustle. Just the gentlest of noises, out of place. Donna thought of stories she had heard: of jungle gorillas who would cart you away; of insects so venomous they would give you a tropical disease that would last for the rest of your life; of bugs that laid eggs inside the skin, that would grow and hatch into worms inside you. It was beautiful, but so, so deadly too.

The rustle grew closer. Oh Lord, that was all she needed. Snake, she thought. Anaconda. Huge, huge snake that would engulf them entirely in their jaws, digest them, burn their bodies down through acid then chew on the remains.

She started to tremble a little bit. What was the best thing to do? Run? But they were fast, weren't they? Fast and vast and on their home territory. Could Fief hit things with a rock this time?

'Whatever it is,' she whispered. 'Forget what I said about not hurting the animals. We might... I mean, it's self-defence. I think we'll have to.'

Fief nodded severely. 'Perhaps it will slip past,' he whispered. 'Don't move. It's vibrations that attract them.'

That didn't help Donna, who was trembling enough to cause an earthquake. Also, she thought sadly of her soaked pyjamas. Any creature that could smell would find its way to her pretty sharpish. Could snakes smell?

And darkness was falling minute by minute.

She saw it, quick as lightning, darting out of the trees. A huge green snake, the largest thing she'd ever seen, thrusting itself towards her.

She forgot the admonitions to keep calm; how proud she was of being brave; how determined she was to keep on. She forgot everything but the very base of her lizard brain, which, for some evolutionary throwback reason of its own, made her scream and scream like she had never screamed before.

She screamed like a child at their own birthday party who'd just lost pass the parcel; she screamed like a silent film star who'd just been given their shot at talkies, tied to a railway track. She screamed so loudly the cockatoos flew on and never came back to that part of the jungle, which had been their home for several generations. A previously undiscovered local tribe, who had also seen the terrible train accident, turned her into a myth; a ghost who came the same day as the smoke; with hair burnt red in the fire; who could kill you by the mere power of her terrifying shrieking voice. It's in the anthropological literature; you can look it up.

The great beast twisted its coils around her and threw her into the air, up, up, and beyond the treeline, catapulting her into the clear blue sky, then swinging back again, brushing the leaves, startling the remaining birds, and still Donna screamed on.

'Please,' came a familiar voice at her ear. 'Seriously, any time you feel like stopping that is absolutely fine. I'm not saying I have unusually sensitive hearing, but I think I'm bleeding…'

The vine – which was what it was – kept on swinging through the trees back and forth, gradually slowing. The Doctor put Donna's hands on it, to stop her trying to claw off his face.

'Hold on to that, please.'

'You're… you're a snake!' said Donna hoarsely as they swung onwards.

'I'm on the thin side,' allowed the Doctor.

'No, no, I mean I thought you were an actual snake!' She hurled her arms around him in delight. 'You're alive! And not a snake!'

'I *know*! Brilliant!'

They swung happily in the air together as the vine slowed down.

'How did you get off the train? Was it a parachute? Did you use my parachute idea?'

'Might have.'

'Aha!'

The Doctor glanced down as the vine came to land in a different clearing, some way from where he'd grabbed her. 'Right, let's get you away from that man. He's far more dangerous than a snake, I promise.' He stepped off the vine lightly. 'Oh, I do like doing that,' he said, grinning. Then he turned to Donna. 'Why are you all wet?'

'Because we're in the middle of a steamy jungle. Why *aren't* you all wet? You're wearing a *suit*.'

'Hmm,' said the Doctor, looking around. 'Come on. There's no time to waste.' He pulled the little origami map from his pocket.

'Wait,' said Donna. 'Fief. Are we just leaving him?'

'I think he can look after himself, don't you?'

Donna thought about it. 'It's weird: he doesn't seem evil,' she said.

'He isn't,' said the Doctor. 'He's purely rational. Which makes him far, far more dangerous. Baddies... they're swayed by things. Emotions. Anger, craziness: stuff which makes them careless. Panic, which makes them make mistakes. But Cadmians: they just do stuff. They don't let much get in their way.'

'How? I mean are they born like that?'

The Doctor shook his head. 'Did you see his earpiece?'

'Yeah. I thought it might be connecting him to his boss.'

The Doctor shook his head. 'No. Cadmians are partly made of sound. They're raised in sound fields.'

'They're made of music?'

'It's not music, no. Music's all about emotion. Quite the opposite. But it is a binding force. They're all tuned in to the same frequency all the time. Promotes suggestibility. Keeps the peace.'

'Oh,' said Donna. 'No wonder their parties are terrible.'

'Quite.' The Doctor licked his finger and stuck it in the air. 'Right, come on, Miss Noble, it's not that far for us. A few days' hard hiking in that direction.'

A faint smile played on his lips. Donna looked at the Doctor and he looked straight back at her with an innocent expression.

'Don't say it again,' said Donna in a warning voice.

'What?'

'Don't say it.'

'I didn't say anything!' His grin was breaking through.

'You're thinking it though.'

He grinned again. 'Maybe I think a lot of things.'

'You're thinking I would have liked the TARDIS here,' said Donna.

'That might be one of the things.'

'You're thinking, I will never ever listen to Donna's advice ever again.'

'You know, you may want to conserve your energies. It's a really bracing hike.' He sauntered on, casually, taking long strides.

Donna shouted after him. 'You know, Fief saved me from a crocodile. Could you have saved me from a crocodile?'

'Yeah,' he said. 'I'd have talked him out of it. Just a dialect of parseltongue really. Less sibilant, obviously.'

He marched confidently on into the jungle.

Chapter
Thirty

Donna was dropping on her feet by the time it got too dark to really see their way any further.

There was the occasional rustle in the foliage behind them. She wondered if it were a beast, or Fief, calmly following them. She thought again of him squeezing the aloe plant onto her bites, which not only still didn't itch, but seemed to have kept the other insects away from her.

She was very grateful for the sun going down and the heat going out of the day, but the air was still warm and wet. She wanted nothing more than a shower. And a bed. A warm, cosy bed with clean white sheets and a soft white duvet, and tight hospital corners, somewhere she could snuggle into, all clean, in fresh pyjamas... Then she opened her eyes again and realised she was stumbling through a jungle a million miles from everything she held dear; from every sign of civilisation. She realised as she exhaustedly put one foot after another that after several long-haul flights, an almost sleepless night, an accident and a long hike, she was beyond tired; that she was falling asleep on her feet. She knew if she sat down, even for a moment, she would simply curl up on the damp ground.

She pulled out her phone from her pyjama pocket. It was miraculously unharmed so far.

'Seriously?' said the Doctor. 'Are you checking your "likes" for your pyjamas? Are you going to take a picture of some breadfruit and upload it with the hashtag #nomnomnom?'

Donna frowned at him. 'Actually,' she said. 'My grandfather is in a country where people are unaccountably going mad with fury then dying as a result of a horrible disease. I want to check he's OK. Is that not all right with you?'

'Well you know, if we had the—'

'Don't!' she said.

There were a couple of bars of charge on the phone… but curiously, something else. As she turned to her right, facing north, away from the railway line, there was a tiny beep.

It was a Wi-Fi connection.

'Huh,' said Donna, showing it to the Doctor.

He frowned. 'That must be a settlement. There must be something around here. I didn't think there was much. Or that we'd stumble on it. I was just following my nose…'

He pulled out the screwdriver and aimed it around. Sure enough it too buzzed in the same direction as Donna's phone.

'Oh, well done,' said Donna. 'It's almost as good as my phone.'

The Doctor looked at her. 'You don't just want to keep on walking? We'll get there faster. Unless we take the vines again.'

'No,' said Donna. 'I don't. It's not that... Doctor, I can't. I need to rest. I know you don't. But I do. Not for long, I promise.'

They moved towards the beeping, eventually cresting a ridge. There was, Donna thought, something about knowing that somewhere comfortable might be up ahead – that she was dreaming now of the reality of soft white beds and clean clothes – that made going on far more difficult, strangely, than it had been before.

It was growing properly cold now. The wind dried her damp clothes against her and it was a profoundly unpleasant sensation. The Doctor had given her his jacket, but it wasn't really helping. She could feel her teeth starting to chatter. Normally when people said that Britain had a temperate climate she snorted at them. For the first time, she thought, she truly knew what they meant.

She looked up. 'Sorry,' she said.

The Doctor shook his head. 'No. Of course we'll stop,' he said.

And just as he did so, there was a tiny line of electric bulbs on the horizon, and Donna wasn't sure she'd ever seen anything so lovely; like little stars. Her face lit up.

The approach was longer than it seemed when you saw the lights. With every dip and gully now in near total darkness, there was no path to discover. It simply went on and on burning her thighs, scratching her ankles, every bit of exertion feeling too much.

But Donna had the end in sight, and tried her very hardest, and the Doctor helped, until finally they scrambled up the last hill to the settlement – to find a walled abbey. It looked European in origin, and completely incongruous in the middle of the thick rainforest. On the other side there was a muddy trail road leading in the opposite direction from the one they'd come. Apart from that, it was completely isolated; a church out of time, golden walls, extensive grounds behind; a bell tower above.

Without saying a word, they both followed the structure round to the high wooden gates. Donna realised she was trepidatious. Why was there a church out here in the middle of nowhere? Or, she supposed, perhaps it was exactly where you were meant to put a church.

Anyway.

There was a huge metal bell pull encased in the walls, and the Doctor cheerfully pulled it. A clanging noise went through the air, momentarily disturbing the cicadas and the chuntering noises of the rainforest. There was just the echoing tolling of the bell. For a moment, everything hung still. And then… footsteps.

Chapter
Thirty-One

Donna had expected a monk. The Doctor had expected a warrior.

Both were surprised.

A Brazilian woman stood in front of them, white jacketed, heavily made-up and beaming with welcome.

'Hello!' she said, her face beaming. 'Well, hello there! Come in! Most people take the road, but no matter! Everyone is welcome here.' She looked at Donna. 'Of course you look lovely,' she said to Donna, who narrowed her eyes suspiciously. 'But have you had a long day?'

The Doctor and Donna just stared at her.

'I was just heating up some of our fresh soup,' she said. 'All ingredients sourced on the premises, of course. Would you like some?'

'Um, sorry, where is this place?' said the Doctor.

'Welcome to the Far Hanging Center for Wellness and Spiritual Health!' said the woman cheerily, pointing to the brass plate by the door. 'Are you booked in?'

'Are you kidding me?' said Donna.

The Doctor and Donna looked at each other. Then they burst out laughing.

'Don't tell them your name, you might be barred,' said the Doctor.

'Ssh!' said Donna. 'Do you take credit cards?'

They started giggling again, and the woman smiled along politely.

'We're normally quite exclusive,' she said. 'A complete meditation and health retreat from the modern world. But we do have a couple of spaces free. Come in!'

Inside, what had obviously once been a missionary church, long vacated, had been extremely tastefully updated. There was quiet whale music playing and smart receptionists in white coats. Women – and it was mostly women – wandered about in dressing gowns and fuzzy slippers.

'He'd like to start with a massage,' said Donna.

'Uh, no. I wouldn't,' said the Doctor, firmly.

Inside, there were fairy bulbs strung up around the body of the church – there was a mezzanine balcony inside, with perfectly placed rubber plants and seagrass matting, and a large wooden candleholder, obviously a relic from the original purpose of the building. Across it was a quad of perfectly groomed grass, completely incongruous out here in the middle of the jungle. There was even a tidy orchard to the back of that, on the other side of the wall.

Not for the first time it occurred to Donna how strange it was that she could travel the universe but there were the strangest sights on her own planet, all around. The stone walls were ancient, with ivy and other clustering plants climbing up the outside. The entire edifice looked like it belonged on top of a mountain in Cathar France.

The woman, whose name was Janet, apologised that they only had the smaller rooms left. In fact, the small cells – obviously once belonging to real monks – were comfortable, with single beds and a small side table. Donna gratefully accepted the bowl of vegetable soup and homemade corn bread offered to her – both were delicious – then took an incredibly welcome solar shower, and put on the clean plain cotton nightshirt Janet passed over.

'Ooh,' she said, happily. 'I might have another shot at a massage in the morning.'

'I'll alert the authorities,' said the Doctor.

Suddenly a narrow bed and a clean blanket were the most luxuriously comfortable surroundings she could possibly imagine, and the second Donna crawled into bed, she was fast asleep.

The Doctor walked back into the main area. It was slightly quieter now. Groups of women sat chatting to one another. They glanced up as he passed. He found Janet tidying a sheaf of magazines by the entrance.

'She did look tired,' said Janet. 'I hope I didn't insult her.'

'No,' said the Doctor. 'Not at all.'

'So, why don't you come over and we'll talk through your wellness programme…'

The Doctor looked around distractedly. 'You don't have a local atlas, by any chance?'

'Should do!' she smiled. 'We have a very nicely stocked little library.'

The Doctor smiled ruefully at the thought of libraries as the whale music played on in the background. They found a small quiet corner with odd ergonomic chairs to sit on. Janet brought over a book of maps of Brazil, as well as a glass of foul-smelling herbal tea.

'This is totally detox,' she said. 'Will clean your insides right out. Total detox.'

'I'm actually surprisingly untoxed,' said the Doctor, looking at it suspiciously.

'Everyone thinks that,' said Janet. 'You haven't spent much time in spas, have you?'

'Nooo,' said the Doctor, flipping over the pages, confirming exactly where they were.

'Everyone needs wellness,' she said. 'Everyone needs to feel looked after. To take a little respite from their daily toil. Even you, perhaps?'

The Doctor glanced up from the atlas for a second. They shared a look.

Then Janet smiled guiltily as her phone buzzed in her pocket, and he took the proffered cup as she fished for it.

'Sorry, sorry,' she said, looking at it for a long moment.

'Everything all right?' said the Doctor.

'Oh, I know!' she laughed, a tinkling sound. 'Sorry. We spend all our time here telling people to get off their phones and relax, and here I am.'

'Here you are,' said the Doctor. He sipped the tea – it wasn't actually notably worse than Donna's – and traced his finger up the map.

'So, we have a full holistic programme,' said Janet, pulling out a large clipboard.

The Doctor couldn't bear a clipboard. He looked up to tell her this. But something was odd.

Now, there were two Janets. She was wobbling hazily in and out of focus. He went to put on his glasses, but for some reason couldn't get them over his noses… they wobbled and fell off and then he went to pick them up… and found himself keeling straight onto the floor.

'Inform the Ice Palace. We have the pair they requested,' said Janet to a white-coated assistant who had suddenly materialised behind her.

The softness in her voice was completely eradicated; as if she had taken off a mask, to reveal the true likeness beneath. The phone in her pocket bleeped once more.

Chapter
Thirty-Two

Donna woke up from the loveliest, deepest sleep, completely groggy, happily coming round. The morning sun was coming through the window, bouncing onto the pale white sheets. It was lovely.

She stretched luxuriously like a cat, basking in the sun and the sheer rejuvenating powers of a good night's sleep. And now they were in a lovely place where she could have a good breakfast and check in on Wilf, before they set off again to do whatever the Doctor was so sure it was they had to do...

There was a banging noise. At first, Donna assumed it was the door. She got up to open it. That was odd. It was locked. Someone must have made a mistake. She banged on it. 'Hello! Hello! You've locked me in! Ha!'

The knocking noise came again. She looked around. There was absolutely nothing in the little bare cell at all, just a bed. The walls were heavy ancient stone; it couldn't be from there.

She moved back towards the window.

'Hello?' she whispered.

'I've been knocking for twenty-seven and a half minutes,' came a familiar, modulated voice. 'At as loud a volume as worked without disturbing anybody else. You sleep too heavily.'

She had to twist her body to see the figure out of the window; he was hiding behind a shutter. Blinking in the sunlight she finally saw him: a pair of yellow eyes glinting back at her.

'Fief,' she said. 'You can just come in the main door at the front.'

'You've been captured,' said Fief simply.

'By a spa? Don't think so.'

Donna paused for several seconds. Then she slowly looked round and regarded the locked door. There was, she realised, absolutely nothing in the room that could be used as a weapon or to escape; there was no chair, no sink, no books; nothing.

'Spas! I hate them! They're so evil!'

'This one is,' agreed Fief.

'Why?'

Fief shrugged. 'Money. Lots of it. They've been told to look out for you. Everyone has. Every gas station, every rest point, every station, every village.'

'It was a set-up,' said Donna, miserably. 'Oh, and the Doctor so wanted me just to walk on.' She glanced down. 'Well at least I'm going to die in a clean nightie. Where's the Doctor?'

'I don't know.'

'Well, can you get me out of this window?'

'I don't know if this is a weight-loss spa,' said the man.

Donna gave him a sharp look. 'Fief? Did you just make a joke?'

'Cadmians do not recognise jokes. It is an—'

'Emotional response. Yeah, I know.' She looked at him thoughtfully.

'I have a weapon, but it cannot be deployed without arousing attention.'

Donna ran her fingers round the wooden frame of the heavy window. 'Maybe attention is what we need,' she said.

Fief raised the gun he'd retrieved from the jungle floor and used the flat of it to smash in the window. Donna smiled and covered her hands with the duvet, quickly climbing up to the window. She stood in the frame and wavered slightly. It was a long drop to the ground.

Fief looked at his hand as if figuring out what to do. Then, he held it out to her. His palm was enormous.

Donna suddenly stumbled, catching her heel on her nightshirt, and fell on top of him. He was an enormous cliff face of a man. Not muscular, not exactly; rather as if there were something else under there. It felt more like a carapace than a body, through the thin skin of the clothes he was wearing.

He misjudged her landing, and she inadvertently knocked him hard on the head, dislodging his earpiece, which dropped to the floor. She swung round and landed on the soft grass, her head jerking up as she waited to hear the inevitable alarms sound. Then she glanced up.

Fief was darting around, on his hands and knees, searching for something.

'What are you doing?' she said.

Fief merely grunted a response. She saw, then, his earpiece sitting just next to her and picked it up herself. Fief continued to scrabble even more madly on the ground.

Donna started to run towards the fence. Nobody had noticed them yet. Fief looked up. His imperturbable face had turned terrified, all of a sudden.

'Come on!' hissed Donna.

'I… I can't!' said Fief. There was something in his voice. Something that sounded like… like panic.

Donna held up the earpiece. 'Is this what you're looking for?'

'Give it to me!' He didn't look angry, or pitiless. He looked very, very frightened. 'Please. It's home.' He held out his hand. His face for once had an expression. It was contorted with misery.

Donna was backing towards the trees, checking to see if they'd been spotted yet.

'Please give it back. *Please.*'

'But what does it do?'

Fief looked around. He was patently scared and ill-at-ease.

'What happens if you don't have it?'

Fief stood back and glanced around, panicked. 'I… just… I mean… I don't know.'

There was a noise, as someone unlocked the door behind them. A cry went up as Donna's absence was discovered.

'Oh no! Oh no, they're coming for us!' said Fief.

Donna looked at him. 'Is this what you're like without… this thing?'

Ahead of them was a beautiful orchard, carefully cultivated. It had obviously been planted by the missionaries who had first moved here, hundreds of years ago. They ran towards it, slipped between the trees.

'Oh this is… this is…' said Fief, his golden eyes now wide-open. 'Those trees… they smell so beautiful. Those oranges. And the colours.'

Donna looked at him.

'We have to… run away,' said Fief, twisting his head. 'We have to get away now! They want to do bad things to us! Come on, let's go… Oh, isn't it a beautiful day. I hadn't noticed.' His yellow eyes filled with tears.

'Oh, Fief,' said Donna stopping, filled with pity. 'Oh. Look at you. Look at you.'

Fief stood stock still, his head everywhere, and Donna had to drag him into the trees before anyone jumped out of the window and chased them.

'Come on,' said Fief. 'Let's just go… into this world. Look at it! Look!' He raised his arms up.

They were deep among the orchard trees now; the bright citrus colours, their overwhelming scents mingling in the warm air.

'It's so, so lovely' said Fief. He looked at Donna. 'I'm so frightened. Quick. Let's get out of here. You and me. Can I touch you? Your hair is very, very beautiful'

'No chance!' said Donna, scampering backwards. She looked at the earpiece in her hands. It looked so innocent; just a tiny thing, like a deaf aid.

'What an amazing world… with so much pain in it… and so much wonder…' Fief looked at Donna. 'And you try and help. That's amazing. That's amazing. Please. Let's go and discover it. Together? Can we? Please. Together. Let's… I want to eat… I want to do everything… I want to dance… I don't know what dancing is, but I know I want to do it.'

'No!' said Donna, shaking her head. 'No, we can't. The Doctor's still in there. And the amount of time we'd last without him is about four minutes.'

Fief turned mutinous, like a child. 'But I'm scared!'

A bird of paradise alighted by his head and he looked at it in joy and wonder.

'Whoa,' he said. 'I mean, *whoa*!' His face split open in a huge grin.

Donna looked at him, full of sadness. 'Fief,' she said. 'Oh, Fief. If we're going to get away… you have to put it back in.'

Fief shook his head, backing away. 'No' he said. 'Don't make me. Please.' His voice choked to a whisper. 'It's not living.'

Chapter
Thirty-Three

The crypts beneath the structure were damp and dripping, even when it had to be daylight outside. The Doctor woke, rubbing his head.

'Still alive, then,' he said cheerfully into the dank gloom. 'That's a plus point.'

Janet moved forward, still with the fixed grin on her face, her heavy make-up perfect, her eyebrows tattooed on. 'Oh good,' she said. 'Up bright and early.' She looked at him. 'You know, you don't look dangerous.'

'I'm not at all dangerous. The people who're paying you are, though.'

He shook his head and whistled through his teeth.

He looked at her.

'You know those people who've been dying? All over the world?'

Janet forced a laugh. 'That's why they need to come to a rest and relaxation retreat! Get away from the terrible pressures of the modern age!'

The Doctor shook his head. 'Oh, Janet,' he said. 'If only that would do it.'

'Well,' she said sulkily. 'It's done now. They're coming for you.'

'Who wants to pay you large amounts of money to get me?' asked the Doctor.

'You don't know?'

'I am having some trouble narrowing it down, to be frank,' said the Doctor, rubbing the back of his head. It hurt.

'Well, it is not your business and not ours. I just need to deliver you.'

'I don't think you even know what you're doing, do you?' said the Doctor.

'What, and you do?'

The Doctor winced as he touched a sore spot. 'Fair point,' he said. He looked around the room and jumped up in sprightly fashion. 'Let's go then!' he said, smiling.

Janet narrowed her eyes at him.

'What? I'm patently completely unarmed. You can down me with an unguent whenever you fancy!'

He glanced briefly to the side and wondered if Donna was awake. If only she would create a distraction that would give him everything he needed…

Precisely on cue, there was a crashing noise upstairs. Donna's window breaking.

Janet jumped, startled, and moved towards the locked door at the top of the stairs.

The Doctor grinned. There was his girl.

There was a knock on the door of the cellar.

'Janet…' A voice came from behind it. 'Janet, I think the girl's—'

'Don't come in!' shouted Janet in a warning voice. 'Don't—'

But it was far too late, of course. The door creaked open, just the tiniest bit, and there was a rush of wind and a flash, and suddenly Janet and a young beautician were looking at one other, and the space where the Doctor had been, and the cup of herbal elixir the assistant had been bringing to knock him out again was lying on the floor, landing, perfectly without breaking, spinning on its axis, round and round, gradually getting louder as it puddled to a stop on the stone ground.

'I'm beginning to understand why the ransom's so high,' Janet said. 'Come on, after him.'

The Doctor headed upwards. There was an open staircase around the middle of the main atrium, and he charged up it until he reached the wooden balcony that ran around the old centre of the church; a place for the choir.

White-coated assistants emerged out of several doors. He glanced around the ancient building. Up in the middle, several metres from the balcony, was an old wooden chandelier with the stubs of ancient candles on it. It hung on an ancient chain from the room, heavy with dust; out of place in such a spotless environment.

The Doctor leapt up onto a wooden balustrade, almost overbalanced, but managed to make the jump to the chandelier. He grabbed it, as dust came down from the ceiling on top of him, and swung dramatically through the room.

'Great cardiovascular workout!' he hollered down, as several people started reaching out for him, and a groundsman came in armed with a gun. As soon as he saw that, the Doctor pushed his legs out to swing towards the tower, and hurled himself through the gap at the bottom of what had used to be the bell tower. He left the chandelier and instinctively grabbed the bell rope, which clanged as he swung to the other side of the tower, shinning up the rope to the stained glass window by the great brass bell.

'Oh, I am so sorry,' he apologised to the beautiful stained-glass window. 'You are a beautiful thing. Built in a beautiful place. With the very best of intentions. This shouldn't be happening to you.'

Kicking out, he smashed his way through the ancient coloured glass.

The Doctor blinked in the bright sunlight outside the window. He was high up, standing on a ledge. There were no vines here, but he could see the spa's beautiful pool complex to the side, different waterfalls and plunge pools built in a verdant planted area at the side of the old church.

The Doctor straightened up and gracefully swallow-dived straight into the nearest one, making a perfect arc through the air.

*

'*Seriously,*' he said, surfacing, covered top to toe in mud. 'That was the mud pool? That was the pond? You cover each other in mud? You know, as a thing to do that's almost as dumb as human ransoms.'

The women were starting to charge out of the front door as he pulled himself out, his trainers making a sucking noise.

'I'm not sure this stuff really works you know,' he said scraping it off his face. 'Oh no, hang on. That *does* feel softer.'

Donna had been hidden in the orchard, desperately trying to deal with Fief.

He was taking a bite out of an orange, skin and all. 'Oh, you have to taste this. It's amazing. I've never tasted anything like it. It's… it's like liquid sunshine. Come! Taste it!'

'I will,' said Donna, getting close. She smiled up at him. 'You know, I've always liked a big fella.'

Fief beamed down at her in pure joy, as she reached up, standing on tiptoes, braced herself with a hand on his oddly firm chest and, completely without ceremony, reached up and roughly thrust the earpiece back into his ear.

There was a long pause as Fief staggered backwards. Donna crossed her fingers and hoped that it would work.

Fief straightened up. And took out his gun. 'Let's go and get your friend,' he said, mildly.

Donna blinked, and followed him straight out of the orchard. She chased after him, just in time to see the Doctor sail through the air and bounce straight into a mud pool.

'Impressive,' she said. 'Fief, see to the doors.'

Fief let off a few rounds, and all the women who had been running out of the front door backed off. He locked them inside the wooden doors of the ancient church, then simply waited there, impassively standing guard.

Donna came pelting round the corner as the Doctor saw the women retreat.

'Doctor!' she yelled. 'We've locked them up inside!'

'You're brilliant, you are,' said the Doctor.

'Did you stop for a mud massage? I'm not sure we've got time…' Donna grabbed his hand to make a run for it.

Fief had put a huge plank of wood across the church door, then quickly kicked his way through one of the high stakes of the wooden fence. There would be just enough room for them to squeeze through.

The Doctor pushed Donna ahead. 'OK,' he said. 'On we go!'

As she bent down to go through, her phone fell out of her pocket. She bent to pick it up. It was flashing bright red with a hundred messages.

Chapter
Thirty-Four

'On we go!' said the Doctor again, pushing her a little.

But Donna had frozen, even as those locked behind in the church started to bang angrily on the door. Her face was unreadable as she scrolled through the messages.

The Doctor heard guns being fired from the inside at the old church door. The door wouldn't last long, he thought ruefully. No respect for ancient things.

'What was it?' he said turning back to Donna.

She held up her phone, her face white. 'It's Gramps,' she said. 'He's in trouble. He's in hospital.' She swallowed hard. 'Mum says... Mum says he's having fits of rage.'

Chapter
Thirty-Five

There was a long pause. Eventually, the Doctor nodded. He glanced at Fief.

'You take her down the road,' he said. 'Steal a car and drive down that track. You get her home, you understand? '

Fief looked at him calmly. 'And in exchange?'

The Doctor sighed. 'I can't Fief... Not if your orders are to kill and destroy.'

'I am merely information gathering,' said Fief, completely his robotic self again.

'Yes, well, information gathering didn't help Ji Woo,' said the Doctor.

'No, it didn't,' said Fief, in that straightforward way of his.

There was a pause.

'I'm going, with or without him,' said Donna. 'You understand, don't you, Doctor?'

'We all have our jobs to do,' said Fief, standing up straight. His glasses were back on. He looked like a man you would love to have on your side, and your worst enemy, all at once.

The fact that Donna knew he didn't care which side he was on made him all the scarier. And without the earpiece he was completely and utterly unpredictable.

The Doctor blinked. 'You'll protect her?'

Donna wanted to interject that she didn't need protecting. Then she remembered she was in the middle of a savage jungle and decided that actually a bit of help would be quite useful.

'You'll wait for me?' said Fief.

'Your methods and mine, Fief…' began the Doctor. He looked at Donna's upset face. He took a deep breath. 'Yes. You can come back with her. You may return. But don't think for a moment I will let you kill.'

Fief nodded. 'What proof do I have that you'll let me come back?'

'None at all,' said the Doctor. He moved closer to Donna and sighed. 'I can't believe I'm doing this,' he said gently. 'But have you got your key?'

'Of course,' said Donna, fingering it around her neck. It glowed, slightly, as she did so.

The Doctor smiled. 'The TARDIS really likes you, you know. Always has done.'

Donna glanced around sharply, as the banging on the door intensified.

The Doctor looked at her. 'You fly it back to me… You phone me. I'll tell you where I am. And you bring the TARDIS straight back to me. As soon as all is well, OK? All right?'

Donna's face was a picture of misery. 'But Doctor… What if Gramps has the disease? What if he does?'

The Doctor sighed. 'I don't know. There's meant to be no cure. I'm so, so sorry. I don't know what you can do. But I understand you need to go.'

'I've been thinking about it, though,' said Donna.

'Ah, a doctor.'

'Don't give me that,' said Donna. 'But look. If it's in the bloodstream, right?'

'Uh huh.'

'Well, what if he got new blood. Like a transfusion.'

'They've tried it.'

'They've tried it in other places. With weird green alien blood.'

'Aliens don't have… well, *some* do.'

'Exactly. Rather than transfuse *green sludge*, what about normal human blood?'

The Doctor sighed, then shrugged. 'Maybe… Donna, don't get your hopes up.'

'We've got the same blood type,' said Donna. 'It's his driver's licence. I hate needles, though,' she added thoughtfully.

The calm modulated voice joined in. 'They are coming. If you wanted to go now.'

The door made a loud collapsing noise, and the first woman burst through. There was hollering as they searched the ground. Fief and Donna rushed through the hole in the fence. The Doctor helped them through and watched as they tore down the hill and round to the road.

He looked back then, at a horde of furious venomous people charging towards him, and he felt nothing but pity.

Janet was shrieking, 'Don't damage the goods! Don't!' But these enraged people, who such a short time before had been simple spa workers, were now roused to the frenzy of a mob.

The Doctor closed over the stake on the wooden fence and headed to the back of the property, well away from where Donna and Fief were headed. He threaded through the orchard which was fenced in with barbed wire, something the sonic could easily manage.

He flicked through and resealed it as the mass of fury fanned out looking for him. He could hear their shouts echoing behind him, as the tall fence was resealed unharmed and he carried on steadily taking out the small paper in his pocket – the unnoticed, overlooked seemingly useless piece of scrap paper he'd drawn in a tiny café on the back streets of Gangnam, and looked at it just one more time. He had the fix on his location now from the atlas Janet had given him. He just still couldn't quite bring himself to believe it.

It was a beautiful day, nothing but a single wispy cloud in the sky, the rainforest spreading out before him down the hill and seemingly on for ever. It was glorious. He smiled cheerfully and turned off the dusty gravel track, plunging in to the steamy jungle below. Behind him was quiet. He hoped they would all be able to massage themselves back to a state of contentment.

He did not see the fateful exchange of emails Janet had with the person who was looking for him, even before the people arrived to take him away.

That it went very wrong, very quickly.

There was anger, and things typed in fury, and tempers rising on both sides. Things became very heated.

By that evening, when the Doctor was already far, far away, slipping gracefully amongst the towering canopy of trees, leaving barely the footprint of his shoes on the springy, damp undergrowth, every single person who had been in the Far Hanging Center for Wellness and Spiritual Health was lying dead at the bottom of the bell tower.

Untethered from its moorings, and with nobody left to tie it up again, the bell tolled, ringing out in the hot mistrals that blow across the Serra Garal mountains.

On windy days you can hear it still.

Chapter
Thirty-Six

It was so strange being back in London. In Brazil, Fief had stolen a car without compunction, and driven it competently and incredibly quickly over the bumpy potholed road for nine hours in the blazing sun into the nearest town with an airport, straight past the platoon of guards on the road to the spa.

They had not spoken much. Fief had insisted on accompanying her on the flight, even though she had suggested he stay at Rio airport and she'd come back and pick him up. He had smiled wryly and said oh, no it was fine, he'd stick with her. Now it felt like having a strange bodyguard following her every move, down to the sunglasses and earpiece. Donna tried her best to ignore him.

Donna loved London normally, loved its busy energy. But its energy had changed. It was the feeling on the streets. An edginess. Groups of people eyeing each other suspiciously. As if they were thinking, did you write that? Was that you? Who said that? Are you a troll? Can you infect me? The fear and the pain was breaking out of lonely bedrooms; spilling over onto streets and public spaces.

Sylvia was waiting for her at the gate looking anxious. Donna left Fief on the street corner, telling him to watch out for kidnappers. She didn't need the third degree right now.

'Took you long enough,' Sylvia sniffed. 'Where you been, darkest Peru?'

'Um… Anyway. What's happened?' said Donna. 'What's happened to Gramps?'

'He got attacked by a clutch of young hooligans on the bus,' said Sylvia. 'I told him a million times, why are you going to the library? What do you need those books for? We've got two hundred channels on the television.'

'So he's in hospital?'

'No, well, it was just mild concussion, they checked him out, sent him home. But then –' she leaned closer – 'he started… he started getting these rages. About anything. People on the news. He started sending off letters to the papers. But you have to do that by email now. More and more of them: people in the papers. People who were different to him. Some of them got published, and it just made him foam at the mouth even more… It's not what he's like at all.'

Donna swallowed. 'I know that, Mum.'

'No, you need to know… When I was a girl… I mean, I don't even remember him raising his voice. And in those days, that wasn't usual at all.' Sylvia bit back tears. 'Of course, your grandmother on the other hand…' She turned away, her voice tight.

'Where is he, Mum?' said Donna. 'Let me go. You go and sit down. I'm sure you've been rushed off your feet.'

Sylvia looked a little pale. 'He… he's in the Moverden.'

Donna stood back. 'Seriously?'

'It all got… it got a little out of hand.' said Sylvia. 'There was a… policeman. And they brought his doctor.'

'Why didn't you call—'

Sylvia shot her the filthiest look. 'I did. Continuously. Sorry to spoil your fun.'

'I was out of signal range,' said Donna hanging her head. 'Sorry. I'll go there now.'

The Moverden Hospital was the local psychiatric unit. 'You'll end up in the Moverden, you will' had been the preferred taunt of teachers, back in the days when it wasn't illegal to treat children like that, or stigmatise mental illness.

It didn't, however, take away the uneasy feeling many people had about the place; the nervousness, the averted eyes going past it. It cast a shadow. Donna knew it was wrong to feel this way. But she still did.

The bus took forever to get there, trailing through rainy back streets. From every damp window Donna could see the glowing blues of people on their screens, their tablets and their laptops. Incredible. The threat of death was not enough. Still couldn't get people off the devices that were killing them. She handled the phone in her lap, resisting the urge to fiddle with it.

But then, look what had happened when she'd been out of reach.

She opened it up. She wanted to text the Doctor, but she didn't think he'd appreciate it. Plus, his phone was unbelievably out of date; it probably had an aerial. He wouldn't have the faintest idea what to do with a text message.

Sitting next to her, Fief glanced over. 'We are ready to leave?'

'No!' said Donna. 'I told you fifty times, I'm going to see my grandfather.'

'It's strange,' said Fief. 'To have… Do you not value all life the same? Is every individual not important?'

'Of course,' said Donna. She wasn't really in the mood for a philosophical discussion.

'But you hold some more important than others.'

'Your family is more important to *you*. That doesn't mean they're more important than other people in general.'

'Except they are to you,' said Fief, musing. 'Those two statements can't both be true.'

Donna turned to him. 'Don't you have a mother, Fief?'

Fief shrugged. 'I was a Cadmian child,' he said. 'We are part of one thing.'

'And you don't get sad when another Cadmian dies? Like, at all?'

'But there will always be another one. The wind always blows in the sound fields.'

'Well, I'll never get another grandfather,' said Donna, sternly.

Fief looked puzzled.

Donna leaned her head against the window, still tired. She would have gone and taken the TARDIS to get to the hospital, but she wasn't the least bit confident of driving it and, knowing her luck, she'd materialise in the middle of an operating theatre. She didn't quite have the Doctor's knack for getting out of tricky situations.

There was something else. She didn't want Fief inside the TARDIS until she absolutely had to take him. And even then, she wasn't going to take him. The Doctor always kept his word. Donna felt absolutely no such compunction.

Chapter
Thirty-Seven

The hospital had high walls with barbed wire on them and a gate you had to buzz through. It looked like a prison. They had made an attempt to cheer up the lobby, with plants and bright paintings, but it somehow just contrasted more with the reinforced wired glass of reception. Despite the many, many signs announcing that it was a non-smoking premises, a heavy smell of old cigarettes hung over everything like a pall.

Donna rang the bell at reception. 'Hello?'

A tired-looking woman shuffled slowly up to the window. 'Yes?' she said.

Donna was busy rehearsing what she'd say to gain entry. She wished she'd asked the Doctor for the psychic paper. That would get her in. Maybe claim it was an emergency? How? Maybe get herself admitted? No. That was a terrible idea. She could call Fief in from the car park. Get him to hit a few people. No. That wasn't the answer either. Partly because it was wrong, and partly because they'd all end up in here. She searched her tired brain to think of something. Her voice came out tight and anxious and expecting a 'no' and she had a stab of that insecurity that came to her sometimes; that she was useless.

'I... I want to see Wilfred Mott?'

The woman glanced at her computer. Oh yes. Donna bit her lip. Of course it would be on the computer. And the computer would say 'no' and then she'd have to start... she glanced around the corridor, wondering whether she could just slide in behind one of the staff? Perhaps she could steal a white coat from somewhere? That wasn't illegal, was it? Maybe she could pose as one of the cleaners? Her brain racing, it took a moment or so for her to hear the woman behind the heavy glass.

'Of course. He's on Daffodil.'

Daffodil, it transpired, was the name of the ward. The woman made Donna sign in and show some ID, then buzzed her through quite cheerfully. Donna felt like apologising to her for her plans to tie her up and make a run for it but instead headed off warily into the depths of the hospital.

It was just a place, after all. The corridors, save for staff walking purposefully up and down, were empty. Occasionally there would be a room – the door closed; again the reinforced glass – with people in, sitting, staring blankly at the television. Many people looked unhappy, but then, they were watching *Homes Under the Hammer*.

Donna felt ashamed of herself for being so scared. She'd walked into plenty of environments stranger and weirder than this and not felt the slightest quiver of discomfort. These were her prejudices, no more.

A tiny girl, thinner than a ghost, who looked no larger than a child – but could not, of course, be a child – fluttered past the end of the corridor, staring at Donna with huge wide eyes. Then she was gone.

And then Donna hit the inpatient wards.

It was like chaos had broken out. There was shouting, screaming, yelling everywhere. Pure rage. The worst language Donna had ever heard. And, occasionally, a high-pitched bleeping and the shouts and screams of medical staff as they attended yet another emergency.

The door ahead of her was locked, but it did absolutely nothing to keep out the noise and the panic. She flinched as a huge face suddenly popped up on the other side of the glass, the face a rictus of rage, teeth bared, eyes wide, spittle flying. She jumped back instinctively. A medic came and pulled the man away, and Donna wanted to shout for them to stay away. Stay away from the spittle; from the rage; that it was infectious.

A large nurse came and unlocked the door. And Donna walked into bedlam, heart pounding.

Daffodil ward had been done up in bright summery yellow and green colours. It had a heavy antiseptic smell about it, as if the staff spent a lot of time cleaning up unpleasant bodily fluids, and was a men only ward. There were moans and groans from every room; a couple of beds in each, then a run of private rooms. The imposing-looking nurse led her down the corridor.

'Fourth on the left,' she said. 'Don't agitate him, please. We're trying to use medication to get him under control.'

'I'm not sure you should do that,' said Donna. 'What do you think is wrong with him?'

The nurse shrugged. 'It seems to be a sudden schizophrenic break. Becoming oddly common. Modern life, we think.'

Donna shook her head. 'That's not my Gramps. That's not the Grandpa I know.'

'Everyone says that.'

Donna shot the nurse some evils. 'He's fought for this country. He knows how to control himself!'

'Go and see him,' said the nurse. 'But you can't stay for long: I have to be in the room with you, and I'm busy.'

'Why?' said Donna.

'Because you can't touch him or loosen his restraints.'

Donna was starting to get seriously worried. 'You're kidding?'

The nurse shook her head. 'It's for your own safety.'

Her heart filled with trepidation, Donna followed the nurse down the narrow yellow corridor, filled with the groans and imprecations of the lost.

Chapter
Thirty-Eight

The Doctor stared at his origami globe of the world, still amazed.

From Seoul, South Korea, to its antipodes; the deepest rainforest of Boa, in Southern Brazil. A line. Straight through the centre of the Earth.

The Doctor hadn't been entirely sure if his hunch was correct. The spa had more than proved it for him.

But if it were the case... then it was technology way, way beyond where twenty-first-century Earth should be. Which meant a little helping hand from somewhere else in the universe. Which in the Doctor's long and mighty experience rarely ended well.

He walked on through the night and over the next few days, following the matchstick edge with pin-like precision. He forded a mighty and uncharted waterfall that bounced down like liquid rainbows. He narrowly avoided standing on a previously undiscovered species of toad. He caught the attention of an ink-black puma, which regarded him with untroubled curiosity before they nodded to one another and the puma stalked back into the darkness of its cave.

He felt the tremors, the humming, before he got there. It felt like the ground was pulsating ever so slightly. There was obviously something right ahead. But there was no break in the forest canopy above; no way anything could be spotted by helicopter or satellite.

Then he felt the temperature drop. It was not yet near nightfall, but he could feel it. The wind had an icy reach, even though that should be impossible in the 38 degree heat of the jungle.

And there it was again. An icy tingle. The Doctor moved towards it instinctively. And finally the clearing opened ahead, revealing a sight that, even though he had been expecting it, still took his breath away. He stopped and put his hands in his pockets, his eyes following upwards.

'All right,' he said quietly, gratified and saddened to see his hunch confirmed. '*And the great gate was a knife edged wind*,' he quoted softly to himself.

Chapter
Thirty-Nine

Donna passed the central doctor's station on her way up the corridor. A junior doctor, who looked about 12 years old, was desperately trying to placate one patient whilst writing out a prescription for another. She looked far too young to be there and didn't even glance up as Donna passed.

Heavy security guards were trying to pull two men apart. Even as they did so, Donna heard their voices getting higher and higher, as it seemed as if they were going to turn on one another.

The private room at the end of the corridor was small, but it wasn't the padded cell Donna had been fearing. Instead it was just a normal room, with a window looking out over nicely tended gardens.

Looking at the bed, Donna got a real shock. It was a normal hospital bed – but with Wilf lying in it, the sides up and two leather straps across his body, holding him tightly down. Donna's hand went to her mouth in horror.

'We ran out of humane restraints,' said the nurse apologetically. 'Sorry. We haven't had a crisis like this in quite a while.

'Gramps?' Donna said quietly, entering the room.

But the man on the bed scarcely resembled her grandfather at all. His face was contorted with fury; there was spit on his beard. He was howling incoherently, twisting in the straps.

'Gramps!' Donna ran to the bed, her heart pounding. 'What's wrong? It's me, Donna. What's wrong?'

'You *scum*! I'll show you! *I'll show you!*'

Donna retreated.

The nurse nodded, in a not unfriendly way. 'Yes, sorry. He's been like that for two days.'

'Have you sedated him?'

'Nothing we've found seems to have worked yet. He's had enough diazepam to fell a horse. We've tested him for dementia, but it isn't that.' She frowned. 'More and more drug-resistant cases we've seen coming in. You've seen it out there. We're overwhelmed. We can't cope.'

'It's infectious, you know,' said Donna.

The nurse shook her head. 'A lot of people think mental illness is catching,' she said sternly. 'It's wrong and it's stigmatising.'

'Yes,' said Donna. 'Normally you're completely right. But this is different. It's completely different. Can't you tell?'

The nurse shrugged.

'But it's everywhere!' Donna went on. 'People keeling over! Getting agitated! You must see this is different!'

The nurse shook her head and folded her arms severely. 'Since I arrived in Britain,' she said, 'I've just been waiting for this. All this stress. All this pressure. How much is your house worth? What does your job pay? What's your commute? Only two hours? Mine is four hours. What are you driving at the moment? How attractive is your other half? How fat is he? Stuff stuff stuff, let's go supersize, double portions, double measures, schools, mortgages, stuff, stuff, more stuff, screens parked in front of your kid's faces, screens parked in front of your face so you don't even... you don't even look at your own children...'

Her voice trailed away.

'My only surprise,' she said softly, 'is that it's taken this long.'

Wilf's muffled curses could still be heard from the other end of the ward.

'Still,' said Donna. 'Still. It is... I can't tell you how I know. But it is a disease. And I think... it's a disease of the blood.'

'That's what they used to think,' sniffed the nurse. 'What do you want us to do, let it? There might be some leeches left down in the basement.'

'No,' said Donna. 'But we have the same blood type... can you give him some of mine?'

'He hasn't lost any blood,' said the nurse sternly. 'There's absolutely no need.'

'I'm telling you! There's something in his blood making him act this way,' said Donna.

The nurse looked at her as if she was about to get her turfed out. 'I'm sorry,' she said. 'I realise you're upset about your grandfather. But you have to realise we're doing everything we can to make him comfortable.'

'Well, you aren't,' said Donna. 'Because you have absolutely no idea what's the matter with him.'

'I'm sorry to say,' said the nurse, 'we see a lot of this in dementia patients.'

'He's not a dementia patient! He does the crossword every morning. OK, it's the *Metro* one, but it still counts!'

'I'm sorry,' said the nurse in a final tone that clearly indicated to Donna that she'd been up against bigger and uglier relatives than her and generally taken the upper hand. 'I'm afraid it's time for you to leave.'

'Well then, you're going to have to find me a bed,' said Donna, folding her arms. 'Because I'm not going.'

The nervous 12-year-old junior doctor sidled past. She stopped in the doorway, awkwardly, fiddling with her glasses. She had a long plait down the back of her white coat which made her look even younger, and a soft voice.

Donna gave her the stink eye. If a long-serving staff nurse couldn't shift her, she didn't think this one was going to have much luck.

'Um, Mrs Mott—'

'It's Noble actually,' said Donna. 'There's two ways of being a grandfather.'

'All right, Mrs Noble, if you could just—'

'It's Miss Noble, actually… Oh god, never mind. Look, I'm not moving.'

'No, no.' The doctor shot a quick look at the staff nurse. 'If you could just pop into my office, Miss Noble…'

Donna found herself following, preparing a few choice words with which she was going to let the doc know exactly who she was dealing with here, and why she was very, very wrong to go up against Donna Noble…

'Sit down, please,' said the doctor. The tiny office was windowless and cheerless. There was a mop in one corner and large towering piles of files in another. It looked like a place for hastily convened bad news.

Donna sniffed. 'Now, let me tell you…' she began.

The doctor raised elegant hands, with short manicured nails in protest. 'Please… Please, Miss Noble. Please. I want to help you. I heard what you said to Agnes. We're… You're right. This is completely different from anything I've ever experienced. We're completely overwhelmed. I do want to help.'

Donna looked at her, suspicious. In her experience people saying those words usually ended up in a huge heap of trouble.

'This… blood thing. You think it's in the blood?'

Donna just stared at her, trying to work out where she was going.

'It's just… I have never seen so many cases. So many injuries, so many deaths. We're a psychiatric unit. We're here to help people. But there is no helping them. Our drugs are completely powerless. Nothing is working.'

'That's because it's not a psychiatric illness,' said Donna. 'I keep saying it, nobody's listening.'

'I'm listening,' said the woman. 'I'm Dr Kaur. Asha.'

Donna blinked. 'It's a virus. They have a virus in their bloodstream that attacks them, makes them furious. You get it through the internet.'

The woman shook her head. 'That's not possible.'

'It's not naturally possible, no. That's why it comes via the internet.'

At this the young woman started shaking her head.

'Oh Lord, why is nobody ever harder to explain to than ruddy scientists!' said Donna. 'You know all the science you know isn't all the science there is, right? You know there are things out there, right? Aliens?'

'Well, I've never seen one,' said the woman primly.

'You've never seen a blooming virus either, with the naked eye, but you believe in those, right?'

Donna took a deep breath. She was not going to get angry. She wasn't.

'Look. You show the internet to someone from a hundred years ago and their head would explode.

228

Now there's stuff out there in the galaxy that will do the same thing today. You just have to go with it.'

There was a long pause. Donna wished she'd nicked the sonic screwdriver again, so she could have shown off some cool stuff.

'You know nothing else is working,' was all she could say. 'You know this isn't right, Asha. You know it's weird and strange and scary and nothing you've ever seen before. Why is alien so difficult a concept to understand?'

Asha frowned. 'So why do you think a blood transfusion? We don't even keep blood here.'

'Because it's a virus in the blood. It's OK, I know he's A+. Like me. Give him mine. We can… I'm sure we can dilute it a bit. It's an alien virus that goes round the blood, and it makes you angry. I've seen it. It makes you angry enough to give you a heart attack. To make you do all sorts of things… Please. Please give him some of mine. Can't you at least try?'

The young doctor looked at Donna's outstretched, imploring arm. 'You have good veins,' she said eventually.

'Yeah, whatever,' said Donna, who was trying to focus on what she had to do and not the actual doing of it. 'Can you hurry this up?'

The woman blinked. Then she appeared to make up her mind.

'Follow me,' she said.

*

Agnes the nurse eyed them suspiciously as they went back into the little single room and Asha pulled the curtains around Wilf's bed.

'I'm just going to take a blood sample,' she said loudly. 'Totally routine.'

She efficiently ripped open a plastic sealed unit of tubing with a syringe on the end and expertly hung up a bag on a loop.

'OK, sit down.'

Donna did so promptly, feeling the blood drain from her face. Oh she *hated* needles.

'I'm just going to send it…'

Asha checked Wilf's chart. Donna showed her her NHS card so they could double-check her blood type. Asha paused slightly and took a deep breath.

'This is deeply unethical,' she said.

Wilf muttered and shouted out loud.

Donna couldn't even bear to look at the restraints. 'No,' she said, touching the leather straps. '*This* is unethical.'

Wilf screamed out loud and started to swear, a long list of everything he was going to do to people once he got his hands on them. His hands and feet were twitching, as if desperate to hit out at something.

Donna winced and held out her arm. 'Do it quickly please.'

Asha cleaned inside her arm with an antiseptic wipe, then brought down the needle.

'It's good this kind of thing doesn't bother you,' she said, thrusting it through the skin and prodding it round to find the vein beneath. 'Some people can't bear needles going straight through their skin…'

'Oh, for heaven's sake,' said Donna, biting her lip. 'I have been through so much more than…' She looked away.

'You've gone very pale,' said Asha. 'Ah, there it is! Never my strong point, getting it first time.'

'I think I might be sick,' said Donna.

'Don't be ridiculous. Now I'm just inserting the tube…'

She had inserted the other end in Wilf's arm, who had responded with a large amount of hollering and fairly colourful language.

'Do you need any help in there, doctor?' came the nurse's low tones.

'No, I'm fine thank you,' shot back Asha, working speedily and expertly, as the blood finally started to flow from Donna's arm into her grandfather's.

'OK,' said Asha. 'Well, I hope this is worth it… Oh for goodness' sake. Nurse!' she shouted, as Donna slumped gracelessly to the side.

Donna awoke to cold water being thrown on her face. She groggily wondered when the last time had been she'd woken up knowing where the heck she actually was.

Agnes and Asha's concerned faces were in hers.

'Seriously. You just fainted,' Asha told her.

'I hate needles,' said Donna faintly, feeling her head go around like a washing machine.

Asha blinked. 'You were the one who insisted I stuck one into you.'

'Yeah,' said Donna.

Asha looked at her, her mouth twitching. 'Well, that was quite impressive.'

'Not really,' said Donna, taking a long drink of water. 'It's stupid to be scared of needles.'

'Not *you*,' said Asha.

Donna tried to stand up but it didn't work out so well, and she quickly sat down again, thoroughly dizzy.

'You all right there, love?' came the gentle voice she knew so well.

'Gramps!' she said.

Wilf was looking up at her with tired eyes. 'What am I doing here?' he said. 'The last thing I remember, there were some boys on a bus…'

Donna shook her head. 'It doesn't matter now,' she said. 'How do you feel? Are you all right?'

'I'm very sleepy,' said Wilf. 'And a bit hungry.'

Donna felt a grin spread over her face. 'Well, both of those we can deal with.'

Asha was shaking her head in disbelief. 'I've never seen anything like it,' she said, unbuckling the bed restraints. 'It just calmed him right down.'

'It's diluted the Rempaths in his blood,' said Donna. 'Hopefully it's got rid of them altogether. Yay!'

Wilf was blinking in his normal benign fashion. 'Can I have a biscuit?' he said, sitting up.

'You should have a biscuit,' said Asha to Donna. 'You need all the sugar you can get.'

'Finally, an upside,' said Donna.

Asha's beeper went off.

'I have to go,' she said. 'They're still coming in. But now we have something to fight it with.' She looked at the two of them. 'Blood transfusions?' she said again, wonderingly. 'Aliens?'

Donna nodded. 'It's science,' she said. 'Honest.'

Asha smiled and whipped round, her plaited hair bouncing behind her as she slipped through the curtain and was gone.

Wilf looked at Donna. 'I don't know what happened,' he said. 'But I think you made it better, am I right?'

Donna tried to look modest and failed. Inside her heart was leaping though. 'Yes,' she said. 'It was all me. I am awesome.'

Wilf smiled. 'Stay a while,' he said.

'I'll call Mum,' said Donna.

Wilf sighed as if that wasn't quite as good. 'Donna,' he said.

'What?'

'Oh, nothing.'

'What, though?'

'I was… I was just going to say. Can you stay a while, before you call your mother? But I know, I know. I'm just a selfish old man. I didn't want you to get married…'

'Well, that's lucky, cause I didn't.'

'I didn't want you to move out from living at home… or find some chap to take you away from everything…'

'Can you stop just generally listing all the ways I've failed as an adult? Thanks, Gramps.'

Wilf leaned over and took her hand. 'You've never failed me Donna. You've never failed at all.'

Donna blushed bright red. 'You're my granddad, though. You have to think that.'

'That's not why.' He squeezed her hand. And they sat for a while. Then he let it go.

'Right,' he said. 'Off you go. I'm heading out too. I'm not staying here a moment longer than I have to, but I can hear Nurse Ratchett's footsteps in the corridor. And don't you have some kind of a… some kind of an odd skinny fellow to save? So. Off you pop.'

Donna smiled. 'That's not usually how it works.'

'Course it is,' said Wilf. He lay back on the pillows. Donna kissed him gently on the forehead and slipped out of the side door of the ward; away from the hubbub and back into the silent, eerie corridors of the main hospital, before she had to talk to anyone else.

Chapter
Forty

The icy wind blew across the jungle floor. It was a peculiar sensation. The Doctor advanced cautiously. The normal rainforest chattering had fallen quieter; no birds, or monkeys, not even a cricket. He moved forward, completely alone. It was total and utter silence.

His phone rang.

The Doctor tutted and felt in his inside jacket pocket. He pulled out the old phone and dragged the aerial out of it, despite the fact that he knew full well the aerial didn't do anything, even before he'd sonicked it. He didn't really like thinking of himself as a creature of habit.

'Hello?'

'Have you been mis-sold PPI?' came the voice.

He paused for only a second.

'Donna! Is that you?'

'Of course it's me, four eyes!'

They both beamed, ten thousand kilometres apart.

'You sound cheerful. And slightly offensive. Cheerfully offensive.'

'I did it! I fixed Gramps!'

The Doctor blinked. 'Really?'

'Yes! Who's your doctor now?'

The Doctor smiled, but his face was still puzzled. 'Well that's… Are you saying he's better? That you made him better with a *blood transfusion*?'

'Completely. Sitting up and asking for the latest copy of "Trout Fishing Monthly". *And* they gave me a biscuit.'

There was a pause.

'Amazing,' said the Doctor. 'I truly didn't think that would work. Well done. Can you come and fetch me?'

'Is that it?' said Donna excitedly. 'Have I solved it all and saved the world through my being brilliant and everything? Do you think I'll get a prize? I want a prize. A Noble prize. Geddit? Are we done?'

The Doctor looked up. Ahead of him, in the middle of the great green jungle of deepest Brazil, a boa constrictor lazily hanging from a distant tree, was a huge, incongruous, unscalable wall of sheer thick white ice; a castle, an impossible shimmering cathedral of white.

'Not quite yet,' he said.

Chapter
Forty-One

Fief was standing at the door of the hospital, waiting patiently. Which made him stand out in itself, on a cold overcast day when he was wearing sunglasses. He wasn't fiddling with his phone or texting or checking Facebook. He was just standing. Waiting for her. As if he would until the end of time.

In a funny way – and Donna told herself sternly that he was a cold-blooded killer who actually had cold blood, which was probably yellow – he was reassuring standing there.

Donna had cheerfully left Asha barking orders and marking up instructions on the white board and looking entirely in control.

'Are you ready?' asked Fief as she stepped out of the door, hanging up the phone. She knew it was just his usual, bland way of speaking but in her good mood it sounded gentle; kind, even. She was projecting.

'Yes!' she said, happily. 'So. Are you ready to kick some coffee-makers' weedy hipster arses? They won't be able to chase us too far, their beards get tangled up in their braces.'

They walked together up the Chiswick High Road.

'I need to ask,' said Donna. 'When the Doctor finds this guy – whoever he is – that's responsible for this. What are you going to do to them? And then us? But first them?'

Fief shrugged. 'Immobilise the threat,' he said.

'You mean kill them? Without remorse?'

Fief thought about it. 'Yes.'

Donna shivered. She remembered again the young steward on the train. She couldn't forget how dangerous this creature was. The moment they had fixed everything, he would kill her. Without a second thought.

'You talk about it like it's a war,' she said.

They passed a young woman who was screaming into her phone; really screaming at it. Something about pictures being posted online without her consent. Her eyes were wild; her face completely and utterly devastated.

'I've been told that it is,' said Fief.

'And you're a loyal soldier.'

'Yes,' said Fief. 'Aren't you?'

'I'm not a soldier!'

'You do his bidding.'

'Sometimes,' said Donna. 'Anyway, that's not the point. We help people.'

'So does my boss,' said Fief. 'He wants to liberate them from this foul disease.'

'Yes, but the Doctor doesn't do it by killing people.'

Fief looked surprised. 'So people don't get killed when he's around?'

Donna didn't answer that. She didn't even really like to think about it.

The coffee outlet was busy and still doing great business. They had to stand in a queue.

'Do you drink coffee?' said Donna.

Fief shook his head. 'After the honeyed waters of Cadmia, I find other drinks somewhat lacking.'

'You're disappointed!' said Donna. 'That's an emotion! Something makes you feel different to something else! You've got one!'

'I have a preference,' stated Fief. 'That's not an emotional state. It's a biological predisposition, nothing more.'

'All emotion is a biological predisposition, you nitwit,' said Donna. 'There's definitely something! Something in there! Coffee makes you sad! So, so sad. Can I see a big yellow tear?'

'I have no feelings about coffee!'

'Compared to "honeyed waters" you do!'

'Not really,' said Fief, but Donna simply gave him a look.

'One jumbo very hot caramel macchiato with three extra shots and a biscotti,' she said as she approached the first bearded man. 'Then, you have to get the hell out. And I'll take my coffee as rent.'

The man squinted. 'Oh, I recognise you,' he said. 'The supposed police box owners, right? Well, you are. Dunno what you've done with the wimpy one.'

Donna looked at him. 'That is actually our police box,' she said. 'And you know how the last bloke was completely opposed to violence of any kind and believed in an equal democratic solution to everything?'

She took a sip of her coffee. It was absolutely delicious. She gestured towards Fief.

'Well, this one ain't.'

Fief kicked over the coffee table stand as if it was made of paper. The hipsters yelled. The taller one came at him with some jerky martial arts moves. Fief simply put out a granite fist and let the man run on to it. He dropped like a sack of sand.

'Sorry!' said Donna to the hipsters. 'I really am sorry. Please. Please don't go on the internet and complain about me. I mean that!'

The hipsters weren't anything like as brave as they'd first appeared. Both of them, as soon as they saw Fief split the salvaged vintage wooden countertop in half with one quick chop, made a run for it.

'Call the police!' shouted one.

'They're busy,' said Donna. It occurred to her that she could still hear the noise of sirens on the air. The news obviously hadn't got through yet; the fact that she had discovered the cure. Maybe they'd call it the Donna Noble cure. She liked the sound of that.

The other customers had filmed everything on their phones, but now the fun was over they were dispersing. Donna wondered if it would appear online. Everything did eventually, didn't it? Pain going on and on and on; pain and violence.

She thought again of poor old Wilf, straying into the wrong argument at the wrong time. She hoped Asha could hurry up, get the news out.

She glanced at Fief.

'Don't,' he said.

'Don't what?' said Donna, pulling out her TARDIS key. It glowed, happily, in her hand, pleased to be back where it belonged.

'Don't think about trying to leave me behind.'

'Why would I do that? You'd just hunt me down and kill me.'

'I would do that. But you might think it was worth it if it gave the Doctor a chance to get ahead, and I want to tell you that it would not.'

Donna blinked. 'I had no intention of leaving you behind.'

'Good,' said Fief gravely.

Donna turned the key, which slid in happily, and popped the lock.

'Is this your ship?'

'Kind of. You know. Yeah. Probably. I'm on the insurance,' said Donna cheerfully, opening the door. 'Ta-da! I like this bit.'

Fief walked through the door. Donna followed him. She pressed the console centre button, and the innards lit up warmly and started to move. Donna stood back, grinning.

'Cool huh! Pretty impressive, don't you think?'

Fief glanced around, completely impassive.

'Come on. You can't be an emotionless joy void about the TARDIS!' She leant against one of its carved wooden struts. 'You can't! Not really. Look at it. Isn't it gorgeous?'

Fief took off his sunglasses and blinked his yellow eyes in the light.

'Come on,' said Donna. 'Say something nice. It's awesome, right? If you like you could take your earpiece out and enjoy it!'

Fief still didn't say anything. He touched his earpiece briefly though as if to double-check it was safe. 'I don't want to,' he said.

Donna nodded. 'I see,' she said. Thrilled to be back, she moved across and patted the console top. 'He doesn't appreciate you like we do,' she said quietly, and the console glowed happily back.

'Can we leave now, please?' said Fief.

'Yup!' said Donna. 'Let me just… Why don't you go and have a look around? Just head straight down to the end of the corridor…'

Donna knew without a map, plus a little extra – a little internal guidance – someone would get lost in the TARDIS straight away. It wasn't possible to find your way through it alone; it was an infinity of itself.

Just long enough, surely, for her and the Doctor to sort this out. By themselves. The way it was meant to be. Then they'd go find him and set him free. Somewhere far away. They might even give him a lift home to Cadmia. She totally wasn't doing anything wrong.

'It still smells of coffee in here,' she said approvingly. 'I like it. Right, go freshen up you. It's four corridors to the left, then take the corridor loop.'

'And we're leaving?'

'I'm programming the coordinates now,' said Donna, taking out her phone.

Chapter
Forty-Two

The Doctor walked around the perimeter. There wasn't a single gap in it. It was a completely impregnable kilometre-round wall of solid unbroken ice towering above him. The fact that it was gloriously beautiful didn't detract from its imposing form. It wasn't a palace: it was a fortress

But there had to be a way in. Because this was where the epicentre was; where everything was emanating from. The end of the tunnel that began in the gardens of Korea. Just one little Rempath in the system, multiplying everywhere, then, finally, triumphantly, zipping through the online world, everyone connected to everybody else. Infecting the world. Overrunning them all. There would be billions of casualties. Unless he stopped it.

A fine and fruitful harvest; perfect sowing conditions, straight into the very heart of the worst of an overcrowded population. The Silk Road. The dark web. Unleash a few onto the darkest roads in the darkest, most furious minds of the world – of a teeming, paranoid, over-busy, over-connected world. And let the worst of the internet meet the worst of human emotion and bang: the rest would happen all by itself. Provide a through route; a collection pipe to send the harvest out into the universe. And there you were. A perfect self-propagating business.

It was revolting. And as soon as they had taken everything from this world – as they would; as populations became more and more fearful, as they were doing already; their fear would turn outwards eventually, and the rage would take hold of everyone – they would simply move on to another, leaving what remained of the Earth wallowing in filthy blood. The meek would not inherit it. The meek felt as fearless and consequence-free behind their faceless computer screens as everybody else.

He blinked. Well. Not if he could help it. He took out the sonic and, very carefully, started to carve a small set of footholds in the ice.

It was painstaking tedious work, but he threw up vines to help him pull himself up.

He knew he was being watched, of course. He had felt it. This was precisely where the ladies of the spa would have delivered him. This was where he was wanted all along. But at least he was here on his own terms.

The ice burned his hands as he crawled, slowly, desperately trying to kick with his feet against the slippery surface.

He was concentrating so hard on not falling down, he didn't even notice his telephone slip gently out of his pocket, and slither down the icy slope of the wall. Within seconds, a beautiful bird of paradise had flown past his head, braving the cold territory they normally avoided, to pick up this useful piece of nesting material.

Chapter
Forty-Three

Donna programmed the coordinates carefully and threw the large lever triumphantly. In seconds they would be back with the Doctor, saving the world. She smiled happily.

Nothing happened.

Chapter
Forty-Four

The Doctor crouched on top of the wall, looking down in consternation. There was a rocket down there, but a small one; clearly not built to convey a person, or anyone person-sized. It was a transportation pod, small, hardwearing and very, very fast.

There were two main buildings, both built with open sidings. One was simply a processing factory, with one or two men working within it.

But the other was odd. It was a stunningly lovely perfect example of a colonial mansion: wooden sidings; venetian blinds, in natural wood. It was very beautiful. The Doctor wondered if it had been built or simply annexed. Everything in it seemed authentic, down to the veranda running around the second floor. It looked like a hunter's lodge. The Doctor hmmmed. And from downstairs, inside, there it was, as he had known it would be: the same blue glow he had last seen in the garden in Korea.

The other end of the tunnel. The tunnel that contained the fastest filaments on Earth. Straight through the centre of the world. That transported the internet one way, providing super-fast speeds and services straight into computers… and the Rempaths straight out the other.

It looked so harmless; no bigger than a manhole cover. It was a masterpiece of efficiency.

It sickened the Doctor to see the Earth being destroyed so thoughtlessly; this was simply a by-product of somebody else's problem, somebody else's conflict. The Earth was just raw material for mining; nothing to be thought of, nothing to be mourned.

'Not on my watch,' he thought, crouching there, feeling the cold air swirl around his feet even as the warm jungle air seemed to reach out to meet it, the cold and the warm together; the heat of the servers; the cool of the ice within.

The wall beneath him sloped outwards, bulwarked like a mediaeval fort with supports for the external walls.

He looked once more between the two buildings. Then he simply sat down on his coat, and slid down the ice wall.

He landed with a bump, stood up, and was immediately surrounded.

The men grunted at him.

'Who the hell are you?' said one, who had a bald head and facial tattoos.

'Hello! I'm the Doctor! Could you do some of that taking me to your leader stuff?' The Doctor smiled appealingly.

Another man stepped forward. His face curled in an unpleasant smile. 'I reckon so,' said the man. 'I reckon he's been waiting for you. *Gully!*'

There was a very, very long pause.

'No,' said the Doctor. 'No!'

'Oh, yeah,' said the man. 'He said you'd met. Said you had lots to discuss.'

He grinned and went over and rang a little bell on the beautiful colonial house. The great wooden door slowly started to open.

Chapter
Forty-Five

Donna put the phone down. It was ringing out. He still wasn't picking up. This wasn't very helpful.

'OK, TARDIS,' she said. 'I think we can just have another go ourselves, don't you? Um… Go get the Doctor. You know! The Doctor! Fetch!'

The TARDIS stubbornly refused to do anything.

Donna started pressing some buttons at random. Fief hadn't returned and she was starting to worry, in case he did. She couldn't rely on him to panic and get himself in a tizzy, as so many did when confronted with the endless possibilities and formidable labyrinth of the TARDIS corridors. Knowing him, he'd logically plan a way back through or make a mental map in his head or something. She sighed. She'd only hoped to stall him for long enough for the TARDIS to make it to Brazil, and for her to leave and lock him in. Just for a bit. She didn't want to hurt him. Also it wouldn't do to have him cluttering up the corridors of their nice clean TARDIS; that Visigoth gang had hung around lighting fires for months.

But none of this would work if he made it back here before the TARDIS moved.

'Come on!' she whispered, pressing buttons cheerfully. 'Come on!'

Nothing. She picked up the phone again. He still wasn't answering.

'What are you doing that's so important?' she hissed.

'Gully?' said the Doctor again as he was pushed forward to the door. 'Maybe it's a different one from the one I know,' he said.

Gradually the men had come out of the dark building where they were carrying out their horrible work, and had surrounded him. The door continued to open slowly. A huge, pointed tentacle appeared around the side.

'Maybe it's a different octopus called Gully from the one I know,' added the Doctor.

'He knows you,' said the man.

'Maybe it's a different octopus who knows me who is also…'

The Doctor gave up.

'Hello, Gully,' he said resignedly.

The octopus – or, more accurately, the subterranean intelligent cephalopod from the planet Calibris – was never particularly pleasant to look at at the best of times; his gelid skin, with its poisoned tentacles, and through which you could see his internal organs shifting around unpleasantly; his wide mouth full of pointed teeth; his constantly shifting, crafty little eyes, far too wide apart.

Now he was even worse; his skin was covered in scaly scars.

The Doctor knew who had caused those scars: he had.

The last time he'd seen Gully, the gangster was attempting to blast off from Calibris, the travel interchange planet, where he'd been running a drugs ring.

One drug, the Time Reaver, caused time to slow down for whoever took it. Gully had been shot with a Time Reaver gun just as his spaceship had blown up. He would have experienced the flaming ship burning up as taking place over years. The Doctor couldn't understand how on earth he'd survived. And, as he so obviously had, how on earth he could possibly have survived with his sanity intact. It wasn't entirely clear how much of that he'd had to begin with.

'There you are,' said Gully, his tentacles rolling and unrolling with delight. 'So nice to see you again.'

'Is it?' said the Doctor.

'Oh yes,' said Gully. 'It's something I've been looking forward to for a long time. Well, not a long time as these things go... You and I, we know something of long times, do we not?'

'How on earth did you escape from that ship on Calibris?' said the Doctor, genuinely surprised.

'You see,' said Gully. 'When you have a very long time to think about things happening, you also have time to consider all possible courses of action.'

The Doctor thought about this. 'That makes sense,' he said. 'But why... why on earth are you *here*?'

'Oh, they had my measure on Calibris after that,' said Gully, crossly. 'But I hung around a few taverns. There's always jobs for smugglers, Doctor. And I am a tremendously good one.'

The Doctor nodded. 'I'll give you that, Gully. If you have absolutely no morals or qualms it's almost a perfect world for you.'

'Quite.'

Gully motioned to the other men to part. 'Come into my office, Doctor.'

The Doctor couldn't deny that inside the house was also a thing of beauty. The computing power necessary to transport the Rempaths – and the reason it needed to be kept so cold – must all be in the other building. This house, though, was a 1920s thing of loveliness.

They both looked at the glowing manhole in the middle of the floor.

'Who wants all these Rempaths?' said the Doctor. 'Who wants so many?'

'Everyone,' said Gully. 'They're the most tremendous weapon. Wanna know why it's so lucrative?'

'I'm not sure,' said the Doctor.

'Because you sell it to both sides,' said Gully, his horrible mouth extending into what passed for a smile.

'What do you mean?' said the Doctor, realising even as he said this that of course he knew.

'You spread it amongst your opponent's civilian populace, lose them all to a hideous dark age of howling pain…' said Gully, rubbing two tentacle tips together. 'But…'

'You give it to your own frontline,' realised the Doctor. 'Send them all in to war furious with their feeding virus; utterly desperate for blood.'

'Guaranteed carnage,' said Gully. 'Guaranteed annihilation. No prisoners. Nobody comes home.'

The Doctor sighed.

'And the money is so, so good… I have a lot of plastic surgery to pay for.'

'You are scum, Gully.'

Gully ignored this cheerfully. 'I'm looking forward to being done here,' he said. 'Bit lonely out here. I miss the city.'

'There'll be no cities left the way you're carrying on.'

'Oh, Calibris will never change. Especially when I get back with enough money to buy her. Now. You.'

'Me?'

'I have a plan for you. I worked out how much time passed for me when I was on the ship.'

'You know it wasn't me who shot you?'

Gully didn't know, or didn't care. 'It was four months. Four months of burning up in an explosion Doctor. Can you imagine what it feels like to be on fire for four months, but to never die? Can you? To feel every single cell in your body crisp up? Slowly?

To feel every single tiny impact. To take every breath, over an hour, to feel yourself, painfully slowly, pull the black poisonous smoke into your lungs, knowing full well all that time you have absolutely no way to prevent it, absolutely nothing to do to stop yourself dying, inch by tiny inch?'

Gully sighed.

'So for YOU.'

He pointed directly at the Doctor.

'Ooh yes. It's going to take a while. But that's fine. Our time frame to total human extinction was six months... although I have to say it's going much quicker than I expected. It's speeding up all the time. They don't really need much encouragement, these little pets of yours, do they? They so love kicking off.'

He moved forward, lifting his tentacles. The line of men stood behind the Doctor, blocking his escape.

'Still. However many months we have. You're going to be here, with me. And you're going to be in pain. Not enough to kill you. No. Not quite. Not when you beg. Not when you cry. I might even bring you with me. I trade anything you know.'

He came closer so his side eye was staring straight at the Doctor's.

'You might fetch quite a price. Bit of a one-off, aren't you? Unique. Always a selling point. I'll try not to damage you too much. Can't promise.'

He fingered his own scars with a tentacle.

'No. Can't promise.'

The Doctor stood in front of him. Where was Donna? She should be here by now. He felt casually for the phone just to check – and then he closed his eyes in frustration.

It wasn't in his pocket. It must have fallen out somewhere. In fact, now, even as he felt for it he thought he could hear it – somewhere, far away, ringing. His hearing was unnervingly acute. How could he have missed it before? It was with the chattering birds, high up in the trees.

Chapter
Forty-Six

'*Doctor!*' screamed Donna, several thousand miles away. 'Answer your phone! *And* stop telling me that I'm getting *worked up.* I know I am. For a *good reason.*'

She slammed down the phone, then, breathing heavily, tried to calm herself down. She glanced at her phone. Checked all the news sites. They were still talking about outbursts of aggression. Nowhere was it mentioning her cure or the amazing steps forward that had happened at the Moverden hospital.

She typed angrily on her social media page.

'EVERYONE LISTEN! YOU NEED TO GIVE BLOOD! IT'S THE ONLY WAY TO STOP THIS SPREADING! TO STOP THIS DISEASE HAPPENING! EVERYONE! GIVE BLOOD NOW!!'

And she pressed 'send'.

Almost as soon as she'd finished typing, people started making suggestions. She watched in mounting horror.

'Stop these conspiracy theories!'

'That's what people said about vaccination.'

This spun on to a different thread, of lots of people arguing about vaccination, utterly furiously.

'No,' said Donna. '*No*, this isn't what I mean, *at all.*'

More replies were coming now, thick and fast; sarcastic; mansplaining things to her about how heart disease and mental illness weren't catching actually and that she was a) very, very stupid and b) ignorant and spreading misinformation.

And then, as her post got shared further and further throughout the web – she could see the counter going up in her screen even as she typed – then everyone piled in. The abusers. The people who made big personal threats about what they wanted to do to her.

'The Nazis did medickl expriments too you know' came one. 'Are you a nazi?'

'I'm not a Nazi!!!!' said Donna.

'Neh, she's not pretty enough' came the next remark.

A huge boiling sense of impotent fury came over her. She started to type rebuttals into her social media, but every time she did so, something else came up and made it even worse than before. Before she knew it people were making remarks about the way she looked, about her hair... It was a total character assassination, and completely devastating.

Donna found herself utterly hunched over the little phone, completely traumatised, brain racing; full of fury and rage, deciding what she was going to type next to show them all a thing or two, to make them listen to her, listen to her about this incredibly important discovery she'd made and none of them were listening, she'd make them listen… She typed back, more furious than ever, desperately pointing out to them where they were totally wrong and what right did they have to interfere with something when she was only trying to make things better and…

The world slowed down. She staggered backwards.

She felt it.

She felt a sudden, icy cold finger. Just touching. Touching her heart, almost curiously. If she hadn't known what it was, if she hadn't heard about it from the Doctor, she would have ignored it, brushed it off as a curiosity, or a small thing.

Her heart was pounding, in rage, yes, but also now, something new: in terror.

Was that it? Was she infected now? Did she have no choice?

In shock, she dropped the phone. It fell onto the hard floor of the TARDIS and shattered, the screen becoming completely unreadable, the pixels below smashing and discolouring beneath her. She stared at it. Then, furiously she crushed it beneath her heel.

She held a hand to her heart. It was racing. She leant over the console, both hands flat on it, trying to control her breathing. Slowly. In and out. In and out. She had to calm herself down. Had to. She tried not to think about whether she was infectious now. Whether she would keel over and die in front of a screen – or worse, like Kenneth, go rogue, try and take some of her fellow human beings out with her. She needed a blood transfusion. But if she didn't find the Doctor, it wouldn't make any difference now, would it?

She stared at the broken handset in agony.

Chapter
Forty-Seven

The Doctor was trussed up and hanging upside down. Apparently this let the blood go to the brain and increased all the nerve centres there. Gully had done his research. He was advancing slowly. The mouth full of teeth – so hideous on a cephalopod; so obviously wrong – were bared in a wide mirthless grin. The men had gone back to their posts, locking the door behind them.

'Do you know what it felt like?' said Gully to the Doctor. 'After your little protégé harpooned me? In the ship that was burning? What it felt like,' he said, drool dripping from his lips in anticipation. 'How long it took. How long can we make it take?'

He shot out a tentacle. The poisoned needle at its tip stung deeply into the Doctor's face as he drew it across.

'One,' he said lasciviously. 'I wonder if we could manage a few thousand a day?'

*

It really does say a lot about how exhausted Donna was, and how double loaded with jet lag and emotion that it took her as long as it did.

After searching a few rooms – there was still no sign of Fief. Donna was sure the Doctor would find him, as soon as she'd found him – and if she didn't, did it matter?

With no joy she went back to the console, trying to breathe the way she'd been taught in the one yoga class she and Hettie had taken together. Unfortunately she had absolutely hated the yoga class, the teacher had been a golden-tanned, honed goddess who had looked on all of them pityingly because they couldn't get their feet on top of their heads, but she couldn't think about that just now. Could she get Hettie's phone? She glanced outside. The streets were totally empty. Everyone was in. Hiding from the violence in the streets. They didn't know they'd carried it inside with them.

'Please, TARDIS! Please! Where is there a phone?'

Donna was imprecating the TARDIS. She couldn't get it to move. Not an inch. Surely if she could find a phone she could call him.

07700 900461. That was it, the only number she'd ever managed to remember off by heart in about ten years. She could call him. Wherever he was.

'TARDIS! Please help me. I'm calm. I'm staying calm. I am calm. If only there was a…'

She bit her lip.

'Oh. OK.'

She turned towards the outside of the door, feeling even as she did so on the streets of Chiswick, the streets she'd known and walked all her life, the odd new sense. Something malevolent. Shadows passing behind windows. Who was it typing about you? Who was saying things about you online? Who could you trust?

People cowering in their houses. The corner shop was closed. Somebody had pulled down the shutters, even though it was the middle of the day. As if they were scared. Of looting. Of violence. It was as if a curfew had come down, even without there being a state of emergency.

Yet. Of course. Yet.

She tentatively opened the little box on the front of the TARDIS. The black telephone hung there, outdated. She didn't even know if it worked. It certainly never rang. She picked up the receiver.

Chapter
Forty-Eight

'What would you call it… plantation chic?' said the Doctor, looking around the room. A zebra rug lay on the floor. The desk was broad, made of rare polished wood. A fan spun lazily in the ceiling.

The octopus stung him again. It hurt. A lot.

'I rather look forward to when you stop talking,' said Gully. 'Probably past the next layer of epidermis.'

He shocked the same area of skin again. And again. The Doctor wheezed in pain. It wasn't really the decor that had caught his attention.

'Did you *buy* it? Did you get interior designers in?'

Gully snorted. He shocked the Doctor again. 'The owners were informed they needed to leave,' he said. He lifted up his suckers. 'Now, you're getting used to that,' he said. 'But this, however…'

Slowly, a sticky liquid emerged from the end of his tentacle.

'There's nothing stickier than this,' he said. 'On your raw skin. Oh, and it's acidic. It will stay there.

Pretty much until it burns through. Although it works pretty slowly, I should warn you.'

He laughed a horrible laugh. The Doctor wasn't listening. Amongst the old papers, in front of the ancient filing cabinet. He was looking at the large, black, old-fashioned dial telephone. Could she?

'Come on, Donna,' he said. The liquid had actually hit the side of his neck. He could feel it, gradually, starting to sear through his skin. There was a burning smell. He closed his eyes.

'Only another four months of this to go,' said Gully. 'Or until the refining process speeds up. Then it will just be the death you're begging for.'

Chapter
Forty-Nine

Gully had his tentacle pressed hard against the Doctor's shoulder blade when the phone rang.

His head shot up. He blinked and looked at the phone, obviously completely bamboozled as to what it actually was. The Doctor twisted his head. They both stared at it.

'It's a phone,' said the Doctor eventually, rasping through the pain. 'A comms device.'

Gully scowled and stared at it for a while longer. 'What are you supposed to do with it?'

'Pick it up.'

Gully nervously extended a tentacle. Despite the pain, the Doctor couldn't help it. He stifled a smile.

'Are you laughing at me?'

'Come on, Gulls. If you can't laugh at a time like this.'

Gully scowled even more and curled the end of his tentacle round the receiver, which simply slipped off the other end.

The Doctor chuckled even harder. 'Oh, you're adorable,' he said. 'Tell them you're on the other fishing line. No, hang on... the jellyphone!'

'You will pay for this,' said Gully seriously. He managed to fumble the phone onto one of his suckers. Then, down the receiver, 'Hello?'

'*Jello!*' shouted the Doctor, slightly hysterical.

But the voice on the other end came loud and clear. '*Doctor!*'

'Donna?'

'Doctor! *Help!*'

'Also, let me say to you: help!' said the Doctor, struggling to lift up his head. 'So. I'm guessing you're not outside with a small liberating force?'

'Doctor! Your stupid TARDIS won't fly!'

'But I told you how to for ages! You said you were listening! And I said, write it down, and you said you didn't need to write it down—'

'I'd seen you do it, hadn't I?'

'Yes, well I've seen you put eyeliner on but I'm under no illusions that I could do it without stabbing myself in the eye!'

Back in London Donna hauled the receiver inside the TARDIS door, pulled it to the console and started pushing buttons.

There was a horrifying crash and fumble and the sound of a TARDIS wheezing in clear distress on the other end of the line. Gully smashed the receiver down to the floor in the mistaken belief that this would hang up the line.

'Just press the blue button!' the Doctor was screaming. '*Blue* button! *Big blue button i have told you a million times!*'

There was a heaving noise then a crashing sound.

'Yeah, OK, so that was the big blue button,' said Donna. 'And we're still here! Also, you need to get the lighting sorted out in here.'

'*Enough*,' said Gully. He picked up the telephone and, in a totally revolting motion, threw it into his mouth and swallowed it down in one.

His body was completely translucent, and the Doctor watched, fascinated, as the receiver slid down into his stomach, with much gulping and regurgitating noises.

'The line's gone funny!' shouted Donna. 'It sounds all bubbly.'

The Doctor forgot all about the pain on his skin and tried to think. 'Come on, come on,' he beamed.

He only had to make a psychic connection over the width of a planet. That wasn't far, surely. No distance at all to them. Surely it would pick up on Donna. The TARDIS liked Donna. It liked her more than any companion the Doctor could remember. It rarely sulked or got jealous.

But now. Something was wrong. What was it? What was missing?

There was a long pause. The Doctor twisted himself around, hoping he would see the familiar outline materialising despite itself. Come on. Come on. Gully was coughing and choking like he was trying to cough up the Bakelite and plastic, but wasn't having much luck.

'Do you want me to pull that out for you?' said the Doctor eventually.

Gully nodded, unable to speak, as the Doctor manoeuvred two fingers free of his bonds, took hold of the cord and pulled. The entire disgusting contraption eventually coughed and spluttered its way to the ground with a bang. The Doctor wiped his fingers on the rope, slipping another finger outside.

'Donna? Donna? Can you hear me?'

Gully started coughing. It was not a pleasant sound.

'Gently does it. And pull up the lever. Calm down. Calm down. Breathe.'

Donna took a deep breath and slowly did both things at once and, agonisingly slowly, the central section wheezed into life.

The Doctor shut his eyes. 'Donna,' he shouted eventually. 'Where's Fief?'

'Uh, he's… he's having a bit of a wander about.'

There was a pause. Donna knew exactly what the Doctor would think about this, and went pink.

Gully recovered sufficiently to aim once more for the telephone, picking it up with one of his suckers. Just as he went to smash it against the wound in the Doctor's neck, the Doctor yelled, 'Find him, Donna. We gave him our word.'

The receiver crumpled under the weight of Gully's tentacle. He picked up a razor-sharp shard of ragged Bakelite, and advanced towards the Doctor.

Chapter
Fifty

Donna would never have admitted to anyone that she was scared of the TARDIS's inner corridors. The very sense that they went on for ever gave her vertigo; it always made her feel like she was balancing on the top of a long plunge down into water. She took out her lipstick to mark the walls as she twisted and turned along it. Fear… more fear. It was not what she needed right now.

'Fief? Fief? Come on, where've you got to? We need to go!'

She tried not to let a note of panic creep in, either to her voice or her heart. That feeling she had had when the icy finger had touched her – it had scared her, deep down, deep within. And her instincts – to shout, to kick out about it, to run around demanding somebody fix her. Desperately she fought a battle to control it. She closed her eyes and breathed. She was so, so scared. She told herself not to worry; she could call Asha, get a blood transfusion. She'd be fine.

If she could do it in time.

'Fief!'

She wouldn't panic, or run or get lost, she told herself. She was going to be the calm, elegant, super-organised, graceful head under pressure...

'*Fief!*'

Her voice was rough and furious. She didn't even notice.

Donna charged down a long corridor past a massive sea of ornately carved, wood-latticed Arabian doors, surrounded by ancient calligraphic tiles. From behind some, alluring music played and the smell of sandalwood filled the corridor. She blinked, looking at them for a moment, then ran on, to the right, which was more familiar, lined with roundels, then down a carved stone staircase with a distinct chill despite the ancient tapestry carved around the central pillar.

'*Fief!*'

And the Doctor. He needed her. He wouldn't say it out loud, but she could tell. There was something about the tense pitch of his voice, the hurried anxiety of his tone. She knew he did. She tried to do some deep breathing exercises. They took too long.

At last, she heard the voice.

'Donna? Why are you shouting?'

She found him, of all places, in the ballet studio, with its great metalled north facing windows, and unaccountable view of bustling late nineteenth-century St Petersburg, snow falling.

'What are you doing in here?' she said, looking around. The pointe shoes were, as usual, all neatly hung from nails in the wall; the piano closed, but with the sheet music standing by.

'It looked...' said Fief simply, fiddling with his earpiece. 'I was curious...' He raised his hands. 'It looked like music. I don't know what that is. I wanted to.'

For the oddest moment, Donna wanted to play him some music. Just a little. If there were time... Then she remembered again that he would kill her without a second's hesitation, and the shard of ice in her heart hardened.

'We're going,' she said brusquely.

Fief did not even glance back at the beautiful studio.

They stood at the console. Donna hesitated just a moment.

If she left now... could she get back to the hospital in time? Find Asha?

But what if Asha was busy? What if she was away? Donna thought back to how tortured the Doctor had sounded on the phone. She paused, hesitated over the button.

One second, two. Then she pushed what she had to before she could change her mind, even though every instinct in her told her to run to Asha, scream, insist she was made well again or there would be... consequences...

'OK,' she said resolutely. 'Brazil.'

Fief took his glasses off and fixed her with his yellow eyes. 'What's the matter?' he said, in his neutral voice that could sound kind, if you wanted to put kindness in it.

Donna wanted to cry. She didn't even know what would happen; would he kill her if he knew? If she was no longer going to be useful?

'Nothing,' she said.

The TARDIS started to wheeze its rematerialisation.

Fief was still looking at her. 'You seem somehow perturbed,' he said.

'The Doctor's in trouble,' said Donna gruffly. 'Which means we're all in trouble. Are you ready if I need you?'

'I thought you didn't want destruction?'

'I don't,' said Donna, a steely tone in her voice. 'Unless it's to save the Doctor. In which case I want you to burn down the entire world.'

Fief looked at her.

She blinked twice. There was something in her, something that made her feel strange; ferocious and pale. Something pulsing within her. She did not return his gaze.

Chapter
Fifty-One

The TARDIS wheezed and deposited itself somewhat unsteadily on some springy green grass outside the large ice walls. Donna came outside and pressed her fingers against the strange cold smoothness of the walls. Then she kicked crossly at them.

'Well, this is no use,' she said, getting back in the TARDIS. 'This is useless! Stupid TARDIS, can't you get us inside? Come on! We don't have much time.'

She could feel the frustration growling inside her.

But, she told herself, this was pretty simple. It had to be. Rescue the Doctor then head back to Asha and get a blood transfusion. Asha could do it, she'd work it out no problem. She felt her fingers connect to the wall of ice she could feel inside her. It felt good. As if something was building; something that had to be let out.

She was glad now she had Fief. They would have to be quick.

She slammed the door of the TARDIS. 'Maybe *inside* the impenetrable wall of ice?' she sneered.

The TARDIS wheezed and dematerialised obediently.

'You're Type 40!' said Gully, surprised and unavoidably impressed. He had now commenced on the Doctor's shoulders.

The Doctor winced and glanced upwards, his heart unutterably glad.

'I have never met a Calibran,' he said through gritted teeth, 'who wasn't the most rabid type of engine spotter. Total sprocket nerds, the lot of you.'

'You just don't see very many of those these days.'

'You don't.'

'When you're dead, I shall steal it,' said Gully. 'Or sell it. Can't decide.'

'Good luck doing either,' said the Doctor. He blinked several times. His breathing was growing raw. 'She dies with me.'

'Guess I'm auctioning you off alive, then,' said Gully. He pulled up his tentacle again and ran it across the Doctor's open wound. The Doctor groaned. 'You'd think this would get boring,' Gully added. 'But it doesn't.' He coiled a tentacle tight round the Doctor's waist, rendering him completely immobile and they both stared at the slowly opening door.

'Donna!' said the Doctor, delighted.

Donna surveyed the scene – the extraordinarily beautiful room, and then the Doctor, his head an utter mess of painful wounds, coiled upside down in the gigantic poisonous tentacles of a huge mutant alien octopus.

'Typical,' she sighed.

Chapter
Fifty-Two

'Put him down,' said Donna.

The Doctor frowned. Something wasn't right. She didn't sound like herself. The playful quality in her voice had gone; she sounded rough and bitter. 'Are you all right?'

'You do know you're missing quite a lot of skin,' she hissed back at him. 'And also you're upside down? Oi, Captain Calamari. I know you. And I don't like you. Is this whole mess your fault?'

'I'm just a trader,' said Gully. 'Guards!'

He called for the men. Fortunately, and more by accident than design, the TARDIS had landed in the doorframe and completely blocked the entrance. There was one window. Fief stood by it and knocked out enough of them that the rest got the message. The Doctor winced.

'Put him down,' said Donna again, angrily.

'Nah,' said Gully. He lashed out with a tentacle and caught Donna on the side of her head.

Over her head, a small dagger shot out. It pinned Gully's tentacle to the floor. Fief didn't even turn round.

'Oh, I see you're quite the team,' said the Doctor.

'Don't make me angry,' said Donna to Gully in a quiet voice.

Gully was carefully attempting to prise the dagger out of his sucker.

Donna turned to the Doctor. 'What is there? What do we need?'

The Doctor wriggled. 'Well,' he said, 'if I could move. Which I have to say I'm finding—'

'Don't waffle,' barked Donna, as Gully started to advance. 'Just tell me.'

The Doctor blinked. 'The ice wall,' he said.

'What?'

'The ice wall. If there's something in here that can make ice…'

Donna nodded, and snapped her fingers. Fief disappeared. Donna stared at Gully, not speaking. He had given up trying to remove the dagger, and instead had simply stretched out his leg. It grew thinner and thinner until finally, it snapped.

'That's disgusting,' said Donna at exactly the same moment the Doctor said, 'That's amazing.' The tentacle started to regrow itself in front of their eyes.

Donna hurried over to start untying the Doctor. 'Seriously, couldn't you get out of this by yourself?' she said crossly.

'I did!' said the Doctor. 'My hands were free! I was just moving on to the other bit.' He took a key out of his mouth. 'Look at that.' He tumbled over easily onto the floor. 'Are you all right Donna? You seem—'

'You talk too much.' Donna didn't even mention the weals on the Doctor's skin. She was so furious with him for letting himself get caught like this when there was so much else to do.

The Doctor blinked in puzzlement. This wasn't like her. This wasn't like her at all.

He was just about to swing down when Gully's suckers popped out of the end of his new tentacle. The beast roared in triumph and advanced on them again. He caught Donna with a slash, and she dropped to the floor, in agony, then stood up again.

'I will... I will do things to you that will carve their name on humanity's tomb,' she screamed at him, rushing straight at him, to the Doctor's great surprise.

Exactly then Fief burst through the door, holding an enormous incredibly heavy gas canister. 'This?'

'Yes!' said the Doctor. 'Quickly!'

'Stand back!' said Fief, loudly. Then he looked at Gully. 'Not you.'

And he sprayed the liquid nitrogen straight in the beast's maw.

Chapter
Fifty-Three

The octopus froze rock solid where he stood, a surprised look on his wide face. He turned completely white, encased in the ice that built the walls from pure nitrogen.

The Doctor grinned as they hurried over to the manhole. 'I think he's just chilling…'

'We don't have time for you being funny,' said Donna. 'Do what you have to do and let's get going.'

The Doctor touched her lightly on the shoulder.

'Don't!' she said. 'Just… Let's get a move on.'

The Doctor regarded her with some concern. Then he moved towards the great manhole in the middle of the floor. It pulsed, as before, with some strange, unseen energy.

'Well,' he said, glancing up at both of them. 'Here it is, Fief. Here's what your boss wants finished.'

Fief nodded. It looked ominous, a blue light shining out from under it.

'We have to fix this,' said the Doctor.

'No,' said Donna. 'Fix the humans first, then come back and fix this.'

'But this… There's no time. We have to do this.'

'We go, then we come back.'

'But Donna, what if we can't fix people in time? What if all of the Rempaths get uploaded? What if the feedback loop runs too fast? Then we can't get back to fix it; everything will be destroyed.'

'Bend the laws of time!'

'I can't,' said the Doctor. 'Not here. Not now. If we go off and we take too long, then everything will be lost. There's nothing against it happening. Nothing. It will be us taking off from a bloodstained rock, Donna.'

Donna had tears of frustration in her eyes.

It was growing hot in the room. Even with the little fan turning. There were already droplets rolling off the frozen statue of Gully.

'I'm… I'm running out of time,' she said, and at last the Doctor understood.

'Oh, Donna.' He stood up.

'*Shut up!*' she screamed. '*I don't have time for anyone to be nice to me!*'

The Doctor nodded. 'Can you… Do you think you can keep yourself calm—'

'*What do you think?*' She whipped round and grabbed the – by now completely disgusting – phone that was lying on the desk. 'I can call Asha,' she whispered. 'Tell her to be ready. How long will it take to do what you need to do in the tunnel?'

The Doctor sighed. 'I dunno, Donna. I have to get in there first, take a look; figure out the circuitry.'

More water dripped off Gully. The end of one tentacle emerged from its ice prison. It started to twitch.

'She can cure me,' said Donna. 'She can! She can cure me! I saw her do it. We did it with Gramps. I need her.'

'Call her,' said the Doctor.

Chapter
Fifty-Four

Donna's hands shook as she slowly dialled the number Asha had pressed into her hands.

'Donna… Donna. I've been trying to reach you!' the girl's voice came.

'Phone problems,' said Donna shortly. 'Anyway, look. I… I've been infected. I'm coming in. You're the only one I trust with a needle. I'm coming in… I don't know when, but soon. It'll be soon. Won't it? *Won't it*?' She glanced at the Doctor, who was already kneeling on the floor, starting to open the manhole bolts with his screwdriver.

There was a long pause at the other end of the line.

'No,' said Asha. 'No, look. Donna. I'm so, so sorry. I'm not sure what happened with your grandfather. But the other people who came in infected, the other people who were presenting the same way… we gave them all blood transfusions, too.' Her voice sounded defeated and exhausted. 'Donna, I'm so sorry. They didn't work. They didn't work at all.'

Donna felt a horrible grip of fear. And the icy hand. She felt a flicker of fingers across her heart. Dancing on her. Waiting for her. Waiting to grip.

'What do you mean? What happened to them?'

There was a very long silence.

'Donna, I'm sorry,' Asha said again.

'What do you mean? I showed you! Gramps is fine now!'

'He is,' said Asha. 'But we couldn't replicate it. We gave all our patients blood transfusions.'

There was a terrible dead humming silence on the long-distance line.

'They all… They're all exactly the same. The ones we still have. Otherwise the disease took its natural course… They…'

Donna lifted her eyes to the Doctor who was still working on the cover, as if he didn't want to meet her eyes. Then he forced himself to do so. The expression on his face was so terribly sad.

'It makes me so angry,' said Asha. 'I'm so sorry.'

Donna swallowed hard. The icy finger touched her. She felt it, the whorls and cold loops of its imprint on the caverns of her heart.

'Don't be angry,' she said, her voice scraping as she got the words out past her constricted throat. 'You did your best. And I mean it. Don't get angry.'

Slowly, she replaced the receiver.

'You knew,' she spat.

'If it were that simple, Donna, they wouldn't be the problem that they are.'

'But why did it work with my grandpa?'

The Doctor stuck his hand up through his hair. 'I dunno. Maybe his fundamental nature overcame it? I really dunno.'

Donna's face was distraught. 'But… But I'm not like him! I get cross at stuff! I get irritated at people all the time! You drive me mad when you take your glasses off and put them back on again every five minutes. Either put your glasses on or take them off! Why is that a difficult problem? Just choose a place for your glasses to be and stick to it!'

'Yeah, all right, calm down.' The Doctor was looking at her carefully, his brain ticking over.

She turned and looked at him. 'See! I won't be able to hold it, Doctor. I can feel it. That cold hand… It's coming for me.' She could feel a tear forming in the corner of her eye and blinked it away. 'Oh well,' she said, attempting a smile. 'If I'm looking on the bright side of everything… at least I won't have to get another needle in me.'

The Doctor looked at her curiously suddenly, and stood up. 'Ohhh,' he said.

'What?'

'Ohhhh…'

'Stop doing that, it is *so* annoying. And if you annoy me, I'm going to turn into a Rage Monster, then try and kill you, then die.'

'Ohhh, Donna Noble I think you might have just… No. Yes! No.'

'When I say you're killing me, Doctor, can I just remind youm, *you are actually killing me*.'

The Doctor stuck on his glasses.

'And there you go again!' Donna gripped the chair, her knuckles turning white.

'So,' the Doctor said, pacing round Gully and back again. 'When you had that blood transfusion... you hated the needles, right?'

Donna shivered. 'Can't stand the bloody things. Always have. Fainted. Out cold.

'You didn't tell me that.'

'Well, I didn't want you to think I was a coward.'

'You actually fainted?'

'Big bump on my head and everything.'

'*Yes!*' he shouted. 'Donna, that's brilliant.'

'What do you mean?'

'It wasn't the blood transfusion! It was the sacrifice! The self-sacrifice. They can't just take blood from a blood bank. That doesn't mean anything to the people who donated it, except a mild sense of smugness and a custard cream. But yours. Yours *hurt*. It cost you to do what you did. And you did it anyway. Empathy isn't enough to overcome those little viruses. But altruism... hurting yourself for another person. There isn't a force in the universe strong enough to overcome that. Well, possibly magnetism, but let's not get into that right now. Yes. Yes.' His face darkened just a little. 'That's why getting Wilf to give you your blood back wouldn't work. Is he scared of needles?'

'He's not scared of anything.'

'That's right. He'd be delighted. Wouldn't mean anything to him. Wouldn't work for you. Aha. Aha.'

He paced up and down as Donna watched him, trying to damp down the brief glimmer of hope.

'But we don't have time.'

He grabbed the screwdriver. 'We *have* to stop this spreading any further…'

'I don't think,' said Donna, with a lump in her throat, 'I don't think that will be much consolation to the rest of us.'

The Doctor paused. And looked up. A shadow passed, very briefly, across his face.

Fief suddenly turned his huge head. 'You would save just one, over everyone, Doctor?'

The Doctor looked pained.

Fief went on, in that same calm tone. 'Time is running out. Why would you even think to take the one over the multitude?'

'Because you understand nothing, Fief,' the Doctor said tightly.

'No,' said Donna, forcing herself to overcome the fury rising within her, the need to shout out 'This isn't fair!' To howl the place down. To placate the beast within. 'No,' she said. 'He's right. He is right. You have to carry on. For everyone else. You do.'

She shook her hand out in front of her. She was deathly pale. The Doctor looked at her for a fraction of a second. Fief and Donna were both staring at him.

Then he straightened up.

'*No!*' he shouted, his voice echoing around the room, the geniality gone; the Time Lord fully present; a fire burning in his eyes. 'I say No.'

He whisked around, his coat following him, to head into the TARDIS. As he opened the door, he turned his head and said fiercely, 'Stay here. All of you. *Don't move.*'

Chapter
Fifty-Five

'What is that, a shower head?'

Telling Donna not to move was, naturally, a complete waste of time.

The Doctor bent over the metal device he'd pulled down from the ceiling onto the console top, examining it closely. He glanced behind at her. 'What did I just say? Stay outside!'

'No chance,' said Donna.

She was scared... so scared, and she didn't know what it would make her do. Something within her wanted to lash out, to scream; to hurt someone. She needed to be in the TARDIS, where she felt safe. Safer.

'Can't you just take me back in time? Break my phone?'

'You'd still be sick,' said the Doctor, who had started working on some other dials. He glanced up. Then he pressed a combination of buttons. 'But we can spare a little...'

The screen showed Fief and Gully outside the TARDIS, both stock still. But something else was apparent: the leaves weren't blowing in the breeze; the fan had stopped.

Donna squinted at it. 'Have you just *paused time*?'

The Doctor shot her an incredulous glance. 'Have I just *paused time for the entire universe*? How would I do that, then?'

'Well, I dunno, do I? You do all sorts of stuff. What about that bee parade?'

'Well, no, *obviously* not. Slightly simpler. The TARDIS has sped it up – relatively speaking – in here for us. So we have a little time to fix this before things get worse on Earth.'

Donna felt at her face in dismay. 'Am I going to get wrinkles?'

'Not if you let me get a move on.'

Donna shook her head. 'What if it goes wrong?'

'It won't go wrong!' protested the Doctor. 'Except with that sleepy princess. Which was *one time*. You should go outside. Far as you're concerned, I'll be done in the blink of an eye.' He looked at her and his voice softened. 'It'll be safer that way.'

Donna shook her head vehemently. 'I'm staying right where you are.'

The Doctor raised one eyebrow. 'Better get to work, then.'

He quickly found her an easy chair, a copy of the *Beano* and a cup of hot chocolate, which were the most calming things that occurred to him under the circumstances, and wrapped her up in a blanket for good measure. She kept complaining about the cold.

It wasn't the least bit cold.

The strange metal device had three points, and a small rivet at the back that the Doctor was now welding something to.

'What is it?'

'The less you talk, the faster I get this done.'

'Yeah, but what is it, though?'

'It's… It's called a chameleon arch.'

'What's it do?'

'Doesn't matter,' said the Doctor. He glanced around. 'But what it can do… what I think it can do… If I fix it properly, I can give some blood to you.'

'I don't want your blood!' said Donna. 'Ugh. Weird alien blood. What if I go all strange like you? What if I start talking gibberish and getting interested in… geometry…'

The Doctor blinked. 'Would that really be so bad?'

'What, all of you gabbling on in my head all day? Yeah!'

The Doctor smiled. 'OK, OK. No. I'm not remotely compatible with you.'

'Innit.'

'But this little device here… If I modify it…it can make my blood human. Human enough.'

'You can turn bits of you human?'

'I can, yes… Is that your spew face? Stop making your spew face!'

Donna didn't want to ask the next question, but she knew she had to. In a small voice she said, 'Will it hurt you?'

The Doctor shrugged and waved a hand. 'Oh… you know…'

Donna knew that meant yes. She looked him straight in the eye. 'And will it work?'

'Hope so.' He looked straight back at her. 'I've seen you in one of your moods before.'

'Oi!'

The job couldn't be rushed, however much it needed to be. Donna finished the hot chocolate. She felt restless, like a caged animal. She stood up and started pacing up and down. He warned her to stop; to hunker down and breathe; but she point-blank refused, and he had to work on, occasionally fussing under his breath.

'I'm not just waiting,' she said, in a tone he had never heard before. 'Otherwise... otherwise... I don't... I mean, I spend my life just waiting around and waiting around, that was my entire life before I met you, waiting for some stupid bloke or some useless job or some other way of totally wasting time just to get through the day just to get one with whatever my stupid pointless life was meant to be about... all that time! Doing my nails and waiting in queues and waiting for the stupid lottery numbers to come up and messing about on the internet. That was what my life was!

'And now that's it, all that hanging around waiting for stuff to get better and now it's going to end out here in the jungle! They won't even know where I am! Nobody will even care! Gramps will miss me for a bit, but they won't even... I mean, they'll probably bring cakes in to work for like two days, boo hoo, well, never mind there's always another temp…

'And I won't leave anything behind, and nothing will have mattered and…'

Bang.

Donna found in dull surprise that she had punched one of the roundels on the console room wall. She couldn't even feel it in her fist.

The Doctor glanced up, his face full of compassion, and tried his best to work faster.

'Oh, I'm sure they'll have a thing or two to say,' Donna went on. 'A thing or two about how I was bound to come to a bad end, Nerys and Hettie and all of that lot, I'm sure they'll have plenty to say. Plenty. About how I was getting on a bit, never really made the best of myself, such a shame, ha ha ha. Well, I'll show them. I'll show them.'

'Donna, please, please just sit down.'

She punched the wall again. She found the angrier she got, the more the heat of the fury rose in her the more it was attempting to melt; to heat the angry cold hand she could feel now; not a touch, but a fist; a cold fist was holding her heart in its hand. She went bright red, although the tips of her fingers were an icy white.

'And you're meant to help! You're meant to help me! But I'm not that useful. Nobody even cares when we've all died. Nobody has missed us. I'm not useful. Not like some flight attendant! Not like some stewardess or some medical doctor, or *Rose*.

'No. I'm just Donna! Just the temp! Just baggage. Mum was right all along.'

The Doctor tried to keep things calm, but he knew as soon as Donna's mother came into things, his best intentions would all be for naught. Instead, he worked on the last adjustments, as precisely as he could, as the storm raged on around him.

'Right, you. Come on. Over here,' he said finally.

'Don't you touch me!' screamed Donna. She was now completely out of control and far beyond reason. Her colour was terrifying; her time, the Doctor could see, was running very short.

Suddenly she turned. A great white fist grabbed at her heart. She screamed, then came charging towards the Doctor, claws out.

'I'll show you!' she screamed. '*I'll show you! Arrrrrrgh!*'

Chapter
Fifty-Six

Everything was very hazy. Lights and colours swung in and out. She felt hot and cold all at once.

'You tripped,' the Doctor was saying urgently. 'Don't you remember? You were... jogging. You were taking some mild exercise. OK, you were strolling. OK, well, you'd just gone to get more hot chocolate. And you tripped. Remember?' His voice sounded strained. 'You do remember, don't you? That it was exactly like that?'

Donna looked up groggily. She couldn't quite focus. There was a tube coming out of her arm that disappeared from her body and snaked its way over to his, but he had his back to her. She blinked. She felt sick... and hot, and odd.

His face was turned away. He wasn't looking at her.

Donna closed her eyes, not entirely sure she wasn't about to pass out again. She realised, though, that there was something inside; as if her tensed heart was unfolding, like an opening fist.

She also realised that she'd been holding her breath, and slowly, gently, exhaled as soon as she knew she wasn't going to throw up after all.

'Doctor?' she said.

Her vision wobbled, and she was briefly seeing double.

The tube coming out of her arm… It led to his sleeve, she could see that. But beyond that, he still had his back to her. She didn't understand why. She didn't understand anything.

'Doctor…'

Still he didn't turn round.

'How are you feeling?' he said. His voice was low and tight.

Donna examined herself. It was… The icy finger inside her. It had gone. She could feel that it was gone; that a huge weight of fear and pain was lifted.

'I… I think I'm all right.' Tears were slowly rolling down her face, although she barely noticed them. 'I'm… Oh my. I think. I think… I'm all right…'

She tried to cast her mind back. It was a blur. She felt, though, a strange sense of guilt, and shame.

'Did I say anything…uh, did I do anything…?'

There was a long exhalation of breath beside her.

'I mean, are you giving me the cold shoulder or what?'

His back still facing her was worrying her. She didn't like it a bit. She gently lifted up her own arm to touch his shoulder, but he jerked away.

'No,' said the voice roughly.

Then there was a pause, and then, finally, he twitched and reached over, and his hand gently withdrew the needle from her arm – she barely felt it as he pulled it out – and still, he would not turn around, but she saw his entire body curl up as, with some force, he threw the tube on the floor.

'You all right?' she said gently, as his entire body sagged with relief.

There was a long pause.

'Yeah,' came the voice. 'Give me a minute, Donna.'

There was another long pause. Then he tried to get up, staggered, fell down. And she wanted nothing more than to pull him up, gently, and put his head in her lap, and hold him still until he was soothed, and bathe his wounds and whisper urgently over and over again that everything would be all right.

But that… that was not the kind of thing they did.

She stretched a hand out towards him. Then, slowly, she let it fall.

He jumped up, shaking himself down.

'You all right, you daft prannet?' she made herself say.

'Yup! Yup! Totally! Right. Let's go. Come on, not a moment to lose, you'll get a grey hair.'

And he beamed at her cheerily to show her how fine he was, and she smiled back, although she didn't believe a word of it.

But of course he already knew that.

Chapter
Fifty-Seven

There was no change in Fief and Gully, outside; they had only been away for a split second. But there was no gas left in the canister, and the octopus had started melting more rapidly, his limbs twitching as he came back to life.

The Doctor ignored both of them and ran to unscrew the heavy metal plate on the floor. 'So what's inside here,' he said, 'is a pipe that leads to the other side of the world.'

'That is amazing,' said Donna. 'Right through the centre of the Earth? Where it's all, like hot and stuff?'

'Yes,' said the Doctor. 'Simple mining project really. Simple for other civilisations, not this one.'

'Excuse me!' said Donna.

'What happened to sweetness and light Donna from now on, eh?' said the Doctor, smiling.

'Oh, yeah,' said Donna. She looked at it. 'It just looks like a manhole,' she said. 'I mean, I could fit down it.'

'You never make tunnels wider than they need to be.'

'Where does it come out?'

'Donna! Geography!'

Donna had a think. 'Seriously? Korea?'

'It's the antipodes to here.'

She frowned. 'Well, surely you can't just take the top off? Wouldn't that do something really weird to it?'

'Well, it's not weird – it's just forces. But yes. If you open it up, gravity will cause the sides of the tunnel to drop in because of the pressure. There's a fluid in there that holds the integrity of the structure that has the filament running through it... kind of a jelly. But once you expose it to the air, the structural integrity disappears and... Kaboom. Or splurge. Whatever the noise of a tunnel falling in is.'

The blue pulse of light ran up again to the ceiling. Another billion Rempaths flowing through, heading up through their pipeline into the rockets outside. Another however many credits in Gully's pocket, so he could head back to Calibris and live like a king.

'Won't that do something bad to the Earth?' said Donna.

'Oh yes,' said the Doctor. He went back to work. 'But it can be open for a little while. Any more than a couple of minutes could really cause problems. Then we have to close it up again, let the pressure disperse underground. If it keeps drawing the air in, we have a situation we really don't want. So. It's simple, but it has to be quick.'

*

The last bolt was stiff to get, and Fief knelt down to help him turn it with his brute strength. 'And will this be the end of it?' he asked calmly.

'It will,' said the Doctor, looking up at him. 'You know, Fief, there are kinder paymasters than yours. There are better ways of doing things altogether. But I suppose that's something you have to feel in your gut.'

They tugged hard at the incredibly strong bolts.

The Doctor glanced at Fief's earpiece. 'Why don't you stop the sounds, Fief?' he asked gently. 'Why don't you let yourself feel? Take part in the universe?'

Fief looked at them both. 'You don't understand,' he said calmly. 'You don't get it at all.'

'What don't we understand, Fief?'

'Your futility...' He shook his head. 'And yet I shall do my duty. Return to Australia. Inform my employer that the job is done. For now.'

'You're not interested in making the sick better?'

'People are people,' said Fief. 'Nobody is any different.'

'But that thing in your ear...' said Donna. 'You know it's just a distraction?'

If Fief could have laughed, he looked like he might have done then. He turned to her. 'Distractions. Distractions like computers, phones, television, books. Music. Drink. Drugs. War? Everything to take away actually having to look at yourselves, contemplate your own existence? I think our way is simpler, that's all.'

'You're wrong, Fief,' said the Doctor vehemently. 'You have to experience everything. Otherwise you're not living at all. You have to live in the universe. You have to let the universe in.'

Fief gave the Doctor a long look, with his strange yellow eyes that glowed like a tiger's in the undergrowth. 'Some people…' he said, still with that uneven penetrating stare. 'Some people are so ill at ease with the universe they live in that they run away. They steal away and they run and bounce about it and never cease to give themselves endless distractions, cause themselves endless trouble in case they accidentally have to stop and think about things. I don't suppose you know anybody like that.'

There was a pause. And then, with one final wrench, the bolts were off and the cover lay on the ground.

'Donna, stand back,' said the Doctor. 'Fief, prepare to run. If you stumble, it will suck you in; it's like the undertow of a ship. We cut the filament, drop the manhole cover, then we run to the TARDIS, OK?'

Fief nodded.

'OK. One. Two…'

Chapter
Fifty-Eight

The cover made a great creaking, grinding noise. It was immensely heavy, and Donna had to come round, finally, to help pull it up. As they did so, a great noise filled the air; a hurricane of wind blew around them with a whoosh.

'Get back!' shouted the Doctor as they hauled the lid to the side of the room. 'Get back! Back to the TARDIS!'

They dropped the lid with relief, where it clanged heavily on the floor, and staggered back against the window; every sheaf of paper in the room was flying around in the air, hitting them in the face.

'Back!'

And then, suddenly, the wind changed.

The Doctor shot up. The wind had ripped the very last of the ice off Gully, and he had shaken himself free and, in the blink of an eye, shot himself into the hole; surrounding the filament; protecting it. As they watched, horrified, he started beaming the blue light up again, lighting up his entire translucent body which conducted it up into the rockets that surrounded the ice station.

'I will take it all!' he screamed at the Doctor. 'Oh, the rage in this planet will make me strong. It will come through me! And I will leave you the blasted remains of this Earth! You had better shut us back in! The filament sustains me! I have its power. And once everyone is dead, this hole can collapse in itself. I'll be long gone.'

The blue light sped up, shooting through him. His deranged face was gleeful. The wind whipped up again, faster and faster.

'Put the top back on!' screamed Donna. 'Hit him with something!'

Gully used the Rempath stream to form a force field of blue light above himself, which crackled and rejected all their efforts to penetrate it with heavy objects. He cackled again.

'And if you survive this, Doctor – which I doubt, unless you never use a computer again – but if you do, don't worry. I shall come and find you. And *you*,' he said, jabbing a tentacle at Donna.

The Doctor blinked.

If he took off the force field and cut off the sustaining filament, then that would expose Gully to the same physical forces as the rest of them. Once his entire body stopped conducting the Rempaths, he could disintegrate into the tunnel, then they could put the cover back on before it sucked in the Earth.

He'd need to be held down, of course. He'd be taking the Doctor with him. It was a one-way trip.

'Stand back,' the Doctor shouted at the other two, grabbing his screwdriver to power down the force field. 'Stand back. And as soon as the blue light goes out, you put the cover on. You understand? You put the cover back on. You do.'

Then he looked at Donna.

'You know everything you just said about yourself in the TARDIS?' he said. 'Everything you said at the airport? Every single time you've been down on yourself? Felt that envy and worry and anger and hate of modern life all around you, and turned it in on yourself?'

She stared at him, heart thumping.

'You must know that, to me, you are the opposite of that.'

Donna felt like she was moving in slow motion, as she shot her head round, realising what he was about to do; that he had turned off the force field and was preparing to throw himself down the hole.

'Noooo!' she screamed.

And then Fief turned too, his yellow eyes burning, and suddenly something was rattling, falling through the wind, down at her feet. He briefly, strangely, ran his hand through her long hair, and touched his mouth to her head, just once, then he shouted, loud above the noise of the wind and the screeching insane cackling of Gully; shouted at full pitch:

'I want to live! I want to live!'

He pushed the Doctor out of the way with no little force, and hurled himself down the tunnel, his huge body smothering the monster, and breaking the beam of blue light.

There was a hideous high-pitched scream from the octopus, and suddenly the walls of the tunnel started to suck themselves in and down, crumbling from the sides, as the two plummeted downwards, through the now disintegrating structural gel.

The entire room began to pull towards the hole, the wind a maelstrom, as the Doctor and Donna, bent over, hauled, panting, the huge manhole cover back to the centre of the floor. As everything now – the fan, the telephone – was pulled into the sucking orbit, more and more things dragged in, the Doctor pushed Donna to the back. In total exhaustion, they made their final heave and, finally, landed the manhole back on top of the hole.

The collapse stopped, but too late for Gully and Fief, now sucked deep down below into the guts of the Earth.

There was a distant boom, from an unfathomable depth below as the space below more or less reasserted itself and the laws of physics came to bear, the liquid just about holding its integrity; the Earth not blown apart.

Donna and the Doctor both collapsed on the floor, exhausted. Donna looked around the room, and out at the rest of the world, and wondered what was left of it.

Chapter
Fifty-Nine

'I just don't know,' the Doctor was saying. He was pacing up and down in the console room. 'The harvest has stopped, but I don't know, now, honestly. For the people who are already sick. If you can persuade the entire human race into doing an act of painful kindness for one another.'

'Humans haven't even got the hang of cleaning rotas,' said Donna. 'Or, like, parking nicely. Or sorting out their recycling. Or…'

'Yeah, yeah, all right.'

The Doctor had called up the news reports. There was nothing good in any of them. Those who were angry seemed destined to stay angry. Until they died. Imminently. And there was so, so much anger out there.

'How?' he said again. 'How are we going to persuade people of this? I love humans, but you can be right selfish so-and-sos.'

'Poor old Fief,' said Donna. She picked up the discarded earpiece. 'So weird. Doesn't work for me. Mind you, I did wash it.'

The Doctor's head shot up. 'Hang on,' he said. 'Give me that.'

Donna handed it over. 'I can't hear anything.'

'Amazing,' said the Doctor. 'Imagine a different species from a billion light years across the galaxy daring to evolve a different audio structure to you.' He messed about with the sonic. 'Tell me what he was like without it?'

'Dizzy,' said Donna. 'A free spirit. Cute, really. Like a kid who's had too many E numbers...'

The Doctor glanced up. 'Without the sound fields of Cadmia suggesting he conform to the good of the species.... like a soft wind through wheat. He's been entirely reared, evolved, brought up to be suggestible. To do the calmest thing. Through this. No wonder he was all spun around.'

He blinked.

'Do you remember when you were speaking Korean? And you couldn't find a phrase for feeling proud of yourself?'

'Yeah,' said Donna.

'Collectivism,' said the Doctor. 'The good of everyone over the good of the individual. Taken to the end extent.'

He paced up and around the console, then looked up at Donna.

'Shall we give it a shot?' he said.

'Can't hurt. Can it? Can it hurt, though? Does it have to?'

The Doctor hit his head with his hand. 'You know what I have to do?'

Donna shook her head.

'If I can programme it to send out a signal to make humans suggestible… It'll need to travel.'

'You mean you'd have to send it back out.'

They both looked at the door of the TARDIS.

'Back out through that filament?'

'Yup.'

'That filament you just got Fief to break?'

'Yup.'

'In that tunnel that's only got milliseconds left before it collapses for ever?'

'When you put it like that…'

They stared at the door thoughtfully for a moment.

'Also, what if it turns humans into Fiefs?' said Donna. 'What if it turns humanity into emotionless robots who kill stuff at the drop of a hat?'

'I thought you quite liked him by the end,' the Doctor reminded her. He twisted the earpiece around his fingers. 'I think it's our only shot.'

'What if we don't know how to stop it? He didn't.'

'Well, I don't know. Let me set a timer on it. Just in case.' He looked at her. 'You know, it won't work on me.'

Donna blinked. Then she realised. 'So I'm the guinea pig.'

'Yeah.' He grinned. 'And a lot else.'

She smiled back at him. 'Hey,' she said. 'You know, I just realised that I am in fact so awesome, a completely emotionless man fell for me. A man with *no capacity for love*.'

'Well, maybe you're quite something, Donna Noble.'

Donna thought of how overwhelming all those feelings of anger and rage had been. How empty she had felt.

And how much hope there was after all; and how much there was still to be done. Could they convey that to all those sad, desperate keyboard warriors out there? Could they?

She took the earpiece.

The Doctor switched it on.

'It should just calm your emotions about anything you might want to do. And then render you susceptible. I might suggest things. Things that are good for the whole of society, not just yourself. You don't have to hurt yourself though. There's no one here for you to cure. So. Please. Don't hurt yourself.'

Donna blinked. 'I could probably do with just a bit of emotion calming. After all that.'

'So could I,' said the Doctor. 'OK.' He took her hand. 'Are you ready?'

'You're not to make me dance like a chicken.'

'OK.'

'Promise?'

'Promise. What about doing the cha cha ch…'

It started.

Chapter
Sixty

Oh, but it was quite the strangest thing, the Cadmian implant.

Afterwards, Donna couldn't have told you exactly what it sounded like.

Fief had been right: it wasn't music, not in the sense of a melody or an instrument. Rather, it was a cascade of different memories and sensations that were obviously in her ear, were made up of sound, but she couldn't tell you what the sounds were. The sense, more, of hot buttered toast and a cascading waterfall and waving grass and the sound of familiar, happily awaited footsteps running up the garden path; and a row of shopfronts she remembered as a child; and the sense of being held very closely; and lavender and seawater and running full pelt through a yellow field with her hair shaking out behind her and toes in sand and rabbit fur and there was perhaps a tune she knew, or rather, a tune she thought she recognised, but she couldn't identify, a silvery tinkling of notes reminiscent of something happy and sad all at once and very far away, something she couldn't get hold of, something that she had once had but was now out of her reach, and it made her sad and excited and happy all at once…

An angry, noisy buzzer went off. She blinked back to reality. The Doctor had his arms folded and was watching her with a slight grin on his face.

'Did you feel that?' said Donna. 'Wow! That was…' She blinked. 'Calming. Yes. Yes it was.'

'Very, very impressive,' said the Doctor. 'If we magnify the signal as crowd control… Yes, it could definitely work.' He shook his head suddenly and glanced away. 'Could have done with it on Skaro,' he muttered, mostly to himself.

'How long did you set the buzzer for?'

'Three hours,' said the Doctor.

'Whoa,' said Donna, whisking around. 'How did he ever get anything done?'

'You're joking, aren't you? You went and did about three months' worth of laundry.'

'Did I really?'

'And made this.'

In front of them both was a three-tiered wedding cake with a large piece out of it. Donna glanced down at her finger. There was icing on it.

'Whoa,' she said again, sticking her finger in her mouth. 'Mmm…'

'And…' The Doctor held up his hand to show her what was in it.

'I whittled you a wooden sonic screwdriver?'

'You thought I'd like it.'

'*Do* you like it?'

'Let's just say yes, shall we?'

'Does it work on wood?'

'No.'

They looked at one another.

'This is our only hope,' said the Doctor.

They both looked outside at the tunnel. It was shifting uncomfortably, the pressure starting to disintegrate the floor around it. The Doctor opening it once had mixed it up, had started the terrible creaking of a hole that shouldn't exist; a hole the Earth didn't have the technology or the infrastructure to support.

It didn't have much longer.

'Well,' said the Doctor. 'No time like the present. I'll fix it to the Rempath filament link. You're going to have to close it on top of me, stop it collapsing while I do it. Otherwise we'll run out of time.'

'Lock you in a tunnel that goes right through the centre of the Earth with two corpses inside and collapsing in on itself?'

'Maybe I'll just play that thing again and suggest you do it,' said the Doctor.

'I bet a real Time Lord *could* pause time for the entire universe.'

They stepped out together, holding hands.

Donna glanced down at the tiny piece of kit. 'It really doesn't work on you, does it?' said Donna.

'No,' said the Doctor.

'Isn't it weird being so hoity-toity above everyone all the time?' said Donna.

'It probably won't be when I'm crawling down that filthy tunnel, no,' said the Doctor.

They both looked at it. It was rumbling ominously.

Donna sighed. 'Well, better get on with it, then. Do you want to take off your jacket?'

'No.'

'All right!'

They heaved up the manhole cover, the wind shooting up, faster and more ominous.

The stench was incredible; not just from the bodies in the hot atmosphere, but the odd belching noise from deep, deep down the bottom of the tunnel – except of course, Donna thought, it was simply blackness. There was no bottom. She thought of an innocent-looking manhole in that beautiful garden in Seoul, beneath an old building she didn't even know was still standing or not.

'Will you… If you fall, will you just fall right through?' she asked nervously.

'Of course not!' said the Doctor. 'Oh no, the imploding wall will crush me before I get much further. The pressure liquid is dripping away now, moment by moment. It could all come apart at any time.'

Donna looked at him. 'Well, be careful.'

He lowered himself in, a spare length of the almost translucent highly powerful filament clenched in his fist, the earpiece in his other hand.

'Right. Here I go. Pull the cover on.'

'I don't want to.'

The Doctor stared her straight in the face.

'I don't care.'

Chapter
Sixty-One

The manhole cover found its home with a clang. Inside now it was pitch dark.

The Doctor clambered carefully through the bodies. The pressure gel that Gully had brought with him was oozing away, slowly but steadily, into the walls. There were ominous noises as the material started to bubble away, threatening the integrity of the structure.

He could feel the heat, too, from far below coming up towards him.

The filament had burned through one of Gully's tentacles, although the latent power in it caused the limb to twitch, sharply. The Doctor flinched, but only slightly.

He found the other end beneath the body and started to tie it all together, ending in the earpiece. He was almost there when suddenly the hole belched and wheezed and bellowed in and out, as if he was down the throat of some living thing. He watched as, far beneath his feet, the blue light started to ping and then to flow, and he started to drop, his feet scrabbling against what was beginning to feel ominously like nothingness. He shot his hands out to the side and braced himself, even as bits of rubble started to get sucked down into the hole.

He looked upwards. The top now seemed immeasurably far away. Well. If he could make it, he could make it. If he couldn't, he couldn't. He didn't dwell on the unpleasant thought of a regeneration happening under the weight of the Earth's centre, coming alive only to die, over and over. And he didn't – couldn't – hurry. That would risk forfeiting the plan completely.

Instead, agonisingly slowly, he inched up through the filthy tunnel like a crab, legs and arms hanging on to the crumbling sides, desperate not to miss, holding the earpiece between his teeth and reflecting that he'd been in more dignified situations. At the top, he jammed himself against the hideous pallid skin of the octopus, looking for a way to keep the filament from following the earth and the fluid from tumbling down below.

'Oh Gulls,' he said. And he reached for one twitching tentacle, and squeezed out the last of the sticky, biting fluid that emanated there, and stuck the earpiece and the connected filament firmly to the very top metal hinge of the tunnel itself, the gap between the structure crumbling every second.

As Gully himself was sucked downwards with inevitable momentum, the Doctor banged the underside of the manhole with all his might.

'OK!' he shouted. 'Get me out! Get me out! *Quickly!*'

He pushed it up and aside, and shot out as fast as he could, as the room bent dangerously and the entire building started to tilt and shift, as if stuck in a tornado.

'*Quick!*'

They just made it, heaving the metal cover over in the nick of time, even as the horrible creaking and groaning noises that came from the hole got worse and worse.

As the blue light shone upwards, the Doctor pulled on the end of the filament and moved towards Gully's control screens.

'Oh, how I hate an octopod keyboard,' he groaned. Then he glanced at Donna. 'OK,' he said, clipping the end of the filament into the computer, and activating it.

There was a reassuring click and beep.

The Doctor looked up at Donna with a broad grin on his face. 'You know one thing I *really* like doing?'

Donna shook her head, smiling back with relief. He was completely covered in muck and slime. She'd tell him later.

'I *really* like reversing stuff. Let's reverse some stuff, shall we? Let's do some excellent reversing!'

Everything hummed into life. The noise filled the air. Donna immediately started tidying up the files. The Doctor rolled his eyes. Further away, on the other side of the world, in terminals and computers and smartphones a long way from here, the effect would be massively diluted. But it would still be there, spreading out and beyond, to cafés and offices and lonely bedrooms everywhere.

He cleared his throat, slightly awkwardly and leaned towards the microphone next to the earpiece connector.

'Um…' he said. 'People of Earth. I hate saying that. It's really not a phrase I like. It's usually followed by something like "Prepare to meet your doom" or "The final hour is upon you."

'But it isn't,' he said, urgently. 'This time, I promise you, it isn't.'

Chapter
Sixty-Two

And in small towns and great sprawling eastern cities, in favelas and old communist apartments, in new spanking developments in the rising cities of India and the endless farmlands of the Canadian plains, in small cafés overlooking the pyramids, in groups of young men hawking rugs in the markets of Turkey, in the fury-driven stock exchanges of Tokyo and New York – people put down their phones, as the waves of the Cadmian sounds pulsed over them. It rendered them calmer – less human, yes, more open to suggestion.

And he told them. That they had to do something difficult. Whatever difficult meant for them.

And it happened. People babysat for their neighbours. They sheltered people who needed it. They spent a long time with elderly people who had nobody else. They called friends and family members with whom they had disagreed. They swallowed their pride. They let the other person win. They sat down for long talks with their spouses.

They played with their children.

The keyboard warriors stood up. Stretched. Opened windows. Took their mums out to lunch.

People donated: money; blood and bone marrow; time, experience, attention. They gave each other so much attention.

They apologised.

Hearing it – *feeling* it – the Doctor really wished Donna was there with him in spirit, rather than tidying up with a beatific expression on her face.

Outside the window of the huge creaking house, the henchmen were fixing each other's wounds, and swapping manly hugs.

On the computer screens showing the world's news, people had turned away from the stories of destruction, and were earnestly talking to one another.

'Oh, Donna!' he said. 'Look at me! Look at me! I'm saving the world with good manners!'

He smiled and talked on, watching the screens as social media slowed to a trickle and then a halt. Then, with a few more keystrokes, he rebooted it, sent a knockout pulse down the filament to every connected device on Earth.

'Go on, have a reboot,' he said. 'It'll take you a while. Let's just call it healing time.' He looked again at the screens. 'That is a pleasing amount of cake-baking going on,' he noted approvingly.

The entire building now was creaking and moving from side to side on the nearly collapsed fault line of the tunnel. It couldn't last much longer.

He reluctantly opened the manhole for the last time, and neatly sliced the whole thing off. The path was closed.

As the wind dropped, he grabbed Donna, and they slipped back into the TARDIS and took off, before the entire building collapsed in on itself, sealing up the hole through the world, leaving merely a barren space in the jungle.

The clean scar of the wound.

Chapter
Sixty-Three

'I won't be long,' Donna was saying. 'I'll see you back at the TARDIS later, yeah?'

She ran up the white steps to Hettie's grand house. She'd picked up a bottle of prosecco at the corner shop. The Doctor waved her off.

Inside there was the noise of charging footsteps and shouting; some laughter; much chaos. Donna had to ring the bell twice before anyone heard her. Finally, Hettie appeared, her normally immaculate hair tumbling curling and wild around her shoulders.

'Don!' She enfolded her in a big hug. 'Don, I am... I am so...'

Donna shook her head. 'Doesn't matter.'

The twins came rushing up to see her and she hugged them.

'Shouldn't they be at Mandarin class or something?' said Donna, handing over the bottle.

'Oh, sod that,' said Hettie. 'Come in. Please. I want to hear all your news. Have you met any nice men?'

Donna followed her through into her sitting room. It had got much messier, much more dishevelled. She couldn't see a laptop anywhere.

'All the men I meet,' she said, 'are weird like you wouldn't believe. I mean. Seriously. You actually wouldn't believe it.'

Hettie giggled. 'Seriously? Oh, Cam may have been around for a while, but I still like him.'

To Donna's amazement, Hettie's sweet tall husband walked through, waving a hand.

'He's home! I thought he was never home!'

'I know,' said Hettie. 'We needed some changes around here. He turned down a promotion. Even though it really hurt his career. I mean, practically killed it. It was agony for him. But…'

Donna watched as Cameron picked up the twins one after another and tossed them in the air as they screamed and giggled frantically. 'It seems to be working out OK,' she said.

'It does,' said Hettie. 'Let's go into the kitchen… As long as you don't mind me getting distracted by the children every two seconds.'

'I don't mind that at all,' said Donna truthfully.

'And what about these men?'

'Space cadets! Every blinking last one of them.'

'You should try internet dating.'

'Hah!'

In Australia, the man with skin dry as a lizard's happily put down the phone, and ordered a list of the sixty most gruesome injuries of the Troll Wars to be posted immediately. The finest clickbait.

And of course the '25 Kindest Acts You've Seen Today – number 7 will make you Squee!' Someone would always start a fight on the comments section below that. Guaranteed.

Money in the bank.

Back on the London streets, the Doctor heard warm waves of laughter, cutlery clattering in restaurants; children running about, playing. Dusk was falling. It was a calm, pretty evening, pinkening into night.

London was bustling, quietly; happily; the wine bars were full of people catching up with friends they hadn't seen for a long time, except on the end of a liked photo or a snatched text, which didn't count.

People were embracing; pleased to see each other again in real life; relaxing. Of course one or two of them were taking selfies. It would start again. It always did.

But tonight. Tonight it was a beautiful evening. All over London, all over the world. Before the grind of desperate, attention-grabbing life built up again, this was an evening to simply be happy, to enjoy one another's company and the small joys of life.

Leaves crisped under the Doctor's feet and he kicked them lightly out of the way, passing dog-walking couples holding hands as they strolled underneath the streetlights.

He found himself by the river, watching the people come and go. A few children were getting the very last minutes of light from the play park, giggling and turning upside down. It was so nice, this world. When they were behaving themselves.

He smiled to himself and turned to head back. Donna would be late, by the sounds of things. That was all right. There was plenty to be done. There were plenty of places to go. Home was a consolation for other people who didn't have the choice, didn't have the options he had. He was lucky.

He blinked.

'Doctor! Hey, Doctor!'

Someone was shouting at him from the other end of the street. It was a man, with a bag tucked under one arm.

'Hello?'

'Doctor? Hey! Wait up. It's me. Wilf. I was just walking to the library. I know I could probably get the bus again, but it shook me up, you know? But that boy… His mother marched him round to apologise.' He smiled at the memory. 'He was just a kid, you know?'

'I do.'

'He was very sorry when I made him weed my entire garden. *And* clean out the potting shed.'

The Doctor smiled. 'Well I think it's probably safe to get back on the bus.'

'Yes, but I started walking and… do you know, I rather like it. Feels good for me, you know.'

'I do know.'

'Can I walk with you a little while, or would you rather be alone?'

There was a pause.

'No,' said the Doctor. 'No, do walk with me. I'd like that.'

They strode on in companionable silence.

'I never know what you've been up to,' said Wilf. 'But is my granddaughter all right?'

'Right as rain,' said the Doctor. 'Honestly.'

Wilf gave him a sideways glance. 'I don't rightly know what you do,' he said. 'Not really. Donna tries to explain but I'm just too... I never quite get it.'

The Doctor nodded and didn't reply.

Wilf paced on. 'But she seems happy, Doctor.'

The Doctor thought about it. 'I hope she is. I think she is. Most of the time.'

'Well, nobody's happy *all* the time.'

'No. That's true.'

'So,' said Wilf. 'Thank you. For making my granddaughter mostly, sometimes, often happy. And whatever it is, that other stuff you get up to. '

And the lights of the embankment popped on, one by one by one, lampposts stretching ahead as far as the eye could see, and the Doctor said, 'Don't mention it,' politely, and the men walked on.

Acknowledgements

Thank you to Justin Richards, Albert DePetrillo, Kate Fox, Alex Goddard, Jake Lingwood and all at BBC Books; James Goss in particular (and please never say H/C to me again or we are THROUGH); Matt Fitton; Pete Harness, Scott Handcock; Lee Binding, Paul Cornell, Gareth Roberts; Rob Shearman; Tom Spilsbury, Dr Matthew Sweet; Peter Ware, Mark & Cav; Kenny Smith; Jo Unwin; all at Little, Brown books and Mr B in his eternal patience with that other guy.